HERO

+++
The Billionaire Salvation Series, Book 1
Bella Love-Wins

This is a work of fiction. Similarities to real people, places, or events are entirely coincidental.

HERO

This story is dedicated to love and romance. May reality be better than fiction... one day.

Join my Exclusive Reader list! You are just one click away.

Follow the link below and enter your email address to and get notified for HERO freebies and more titles by Bella Love-Wins once they are off the press.

>>>**Click here to get FRESH Hero freebies and updates**<<<

Once again thank you, I hope you enjoy it!

Sincerely,

Bella Love-Wins

Website: http://bellalovewins.com/

Twitter: @BellaLoveWins on Twitter

Facebook: https://www.facebook.com/BellaLoveWins

Wattpad: http://www.wattpad.com/user/BellaLoveWins

HERO

+++
~ She was hoping for a hero, but never realized who she
would save. ~
+++

~~ Chapter One ~~

"Are you alright?" asked the tall, well-dressed man who helped me up off the sidewalk after I tripped.

I was so embarrassed, gathering up my makeup, wallet, keys and other unmentionables that had fallen out of my purse and spilled just about everywhere.

"Um, yes, thank you," I said weakly, looking back at the street to figure out what had made me slip and fall.

I was already late, and now I was both late and publicly humiliated. It's funny, how we get so embarrassed for some of the stupidest things. I mean, gravity exists, and therefore we fall. Babies fall all the time. And so do kids. But what is the point when suddenly we're embarrassed about falling?

I didn't have time to explore the thought concept, but figured that maybe I might mention it at some point that day. I was in a rush to my part time online radio news station job as a DJ/news reporter.

"You're late, Kate," said George Wilkinson, the station's evening producer, close gay friend every woman loves to have, and all-round pain in the ass.

I decided it was probably in my best interest to ignore him. I was in a bad mood, and he probably was as well. I logged in to my music archive account and started pulling together the music sequence for my shift, which mostly was already done by George, but sometimes he had no talent for understanding what needed to go where. And that was one of the reasons that they accepted my frequent lateness. I knew what to play and I knew how to get the online and phone-in fans engaged.

After graduating from college in Communications and Social Media Strategy, it was the first job I interviewed for. I had already been a college radio DJ and felt comfortable on the air, so I knew this job would be a breeze. That was until I bombed the interview. I think I wanted it too much. It represented freedom from my past, independence from them. Still, I got a call back about three weeks after my interview when one of their part-time

DJs just up and walked out during a live show. That was good for me.

So when they called me in for a second chance, it went much more smoothly. And when they hired me, they had no regrets. I was the one who pitched for most viral song of the week, a social voting online contest, and it boosted our listener numbers by 38%. Mind you, it also increased the number of psychos phoning in and social media 'ragers', yapping about us on Twitter and Facebook. I didn't mind too much when they yelled or sent those messages in all caps that were so annoying. It was great for our ratings.

I stretched my arm out and leaned past George to reach for the shift sequence. He was sitting beside me to cue up the news feed.

"Remember to mention the 'newsrockcontest' hashtag as soon as you get on, okay?" he said as he got up to grab an espresso from the automatic coffee machine plugged in in the corner. Quality, single-serve brewed coffee was one of the few perks of this job.

"I created the hashtag, remember?" I reminded him.

"Yes and maybe you should create a 'Hero for Kate' hashtag so you can find a nice man in time for the holidays."

One of the downsides of the job is that everyone knew your business, and you couldn't help sharing it because you're always in such close quarters.

"Maybe I should take your man, George," I said snidely. George was married to one of the sexiest men in Manhattan. Tall, ridiculously handsome, fit and rich. Too bad he was gay.

"Go ahead and try," he scoffed. "By the way, how come you're not seeing that guy from the fourth floor?"

I wanted to refer to him as *that guy* too. He was a complete flop in bed, pun intended. And it took me a long six dates to find that out.

"Fucking waste of time," I responded as he left the room, and I thought to myself, *good thing I was holding out for my hero.*

Ever since I could remember, I had had this particular fantasy about meeting *The One*. I was infatuated with the idea that I'd meet and fall in love with a hero. An alpha male in a job where he wore a uniform. He would save the day, steal my heart, own my soul and make my life whole. There was just something about a hero archetype that mesmerized me. Their rugged bodies; that proud, cocky walk many of them had; their brute strength, protective nature, commanding presence, and independence like nothing else. I had to have me one of them. For life. And I guess I was keeping myself romantically pure, if nothing else, until I found him.

A hero to me is strong, steady, noble, and compassionate. At least that's what I read in every adventure romance that I've ever read. I wasn't much for movies, but the ones I've watched completely reinforced my theory and desire for one. And what would make matters worse, is the recurring dream I had of him. This one dream that kept repeating over and over again, like one of those broken turntable records my grandpa used to play.

In the dream, I was crossing the street in front of my building, and he would quickly grab me around my waist and push me out of the path of an oncoming car. I would land ever so gently on the sidewalk, wrapped safely in his arms, with his muscled body pressed onto my chest. His blue eyes were powerful, piercing into my soul, with his bedroom smile warming me to my core. The world would fall away like no one was there except him and me. We'd end up on his bed with me spread out on it, calling out his name as he'd make me come over and over again. And after he came, as I'd run my hand through his dark hair, looking dreamily into his eyes, I'd wake up.

It was one of those dreams that you wake up from and wish you could fall back to sleep and pick up where you left off, and have it go on and on. But it always ended at that exact same point. I've had that dream since I was seventeen, and now, four years later, I was still waiting.

And sometimes, I would curse these dreams. If I didn't have them, maybe I would've seen Chad Bridges coming from a mile away. Maybe I wouldn't have romanticized his job as a firefighter. Maybe I wouldn't have gotten so close to him so quickly. Maybe I wouldn't have slept with him on the second date. Maybe I wouldn't have let him fuck me over in more ways than one. And maybe he wouldn't have broken my heart with all of his lies and made me so jaded about meeting my real hero. I dumped Chad, after I found out that he'd lied and cheated on me, with my best friend from college of all people. Once he was gone, I put him in the 'wolf in hero's clothing' category and decided he was not worthy of filling the shoes of the man of my dreams.

George re-entered the room. "What the hell are you doing? Five seconds of dead air, get your news script and talk!"

I straightened up and got to it, realizing I had gotten a little distracted by my thoughts.

"Got it," I replied, feeling a touch guilty.

Within seven minutes the news had been read and we were back to the queued music sequence. George sat down beside me again.

"I've got to keep an eye on you, girl," he said. "You can't let that happen again."

"Sorry about that."

"What's going on with you anyway?" he asked.

"Oh, nothing," I replied. "Probably just a little tired."

It was late November, and the days were getting shorter. The leaves had already turned, and most of them had fallen off the oaks and birch trees in the neighborhood. We'd even had a couple of snowfalls just before Black Friday.

"Well, maybe you should have some coffee because if I have to warn you again tonight, I may have to fire your high and mighty ass. I've gotten enough flak from the station manager and ultimately, no matter how savvy you are in all things social media,

I'm accountable. Keep your head in the game when you're sitting in that chair, okay?"

"All right. Sorry," I replied. "It won't happen again."

But I knew it probably would, because that dream had turned into a lot of daydreaming, and I gotten into substantial trouble for it over the years. And there wasn't a doubt in my mind that I'd probably get fired or run over by a bus one day for exactly the same reason. A distracted, daydreaming DJ was a dead DJ. Ditto for my part-time waitressing job I had had right up until the end if this past summer. The job at the station was still part-time, so I had taken a job as a restaurant greeter at the gourmet Italian restaurant two blocks from where I live. The pay sucked, but the tips were crazy good. It had just become too much, and not challenging enough, so I had quit at the end of that past summer.

"So Kate, what are you doing after shift tonight?"

"No plans. Why?"

"Richard and I are meeting for the Arthur Jazz premier, and we have a couple of extra tickets. Richard has a friend who..."

"Not again George," I countered. "You and Richard are not matchmakers, and I'm not falling for that again. The last time I ended up like a third wheel for you two, because the guy ran off. Honestly, that was not good for my ego."

"Trust me I wouldn't set you up again. And you know the guy ran off because you insulted him."

"It was not an insult," I answered. "It was a statement."

"You told him his shirt smelled like cinnamon and sweat."

"Well, next time don't try to hook me up with someone that works at a bakery.'

"The guy owns the largest baked goods franchise in the state, Kate," George said. "I'm telling you, you missed out with that one. He lives in a Fifth Avenue penthouse. And he's a really nice guy."

"And you would know right George?" I regretted saying it the second after it came out of my mouth. I softened my tone. "Look

George, I know that you mean well, but I'm just not ready for anyone right now. And I will pass on tonight, okay? Oh, that's my cue."

I started my signature radio chant. "Ladies and gentlemen, it's a cold evening, getting colder with lake effect snow in the forecast. You're tuned in to WRFJ 92.7 FM New York, and you're listening to Kate Rock. We have exactly 27 days until Christmas. Time to get in gear, listeners. You know you don't want to be one of those last-minute shoppers, fight the mad Christmas Eve rush, kicking and screaming your fellow man for that last coveted gift on the stores shelves, trying desperately to please those wonderful people you love."

I got into my groove, and the rest of the shift just flew by. George didn't raise the question of plans, boyfriends, dates, or anything else for the rest of the night. He may have been avoiding me after my rant. I felt a little bad, but it was good to have some quiet around the place.

~~ Chapter Two ~~

I was hungry after my shift was over, so I decided to go have a bite at Sabatini's - the Italian restaurant where I used to work. As I walked in, I saw a few of my old coworkers were on shift.

"Hey Kate," said Joy, the hostess who filled my vacancy after I left. She was clearly from the New York aristocracy. She was all manners and breeding. Apparently, her parents had cut her off financially to teach her a life lesson before she could access her trust fund. This job at the restaurant was all that she could find. And it allowed her to stay close to home, and to continue putting the pressure on her parents to give in. Naturally, she was no good at the job, so every time I came by for a meal, she felt a little threatened. "You're not back for your old job, are you?"

"Not at all Joy," I answered. "Lighten up a bit, would you?"

"I was kidding Kate," Joy replied. "But if you'd said yes, for once, I'd actually be happy. It's a zoo in here."

"Well, it's all-you-can-eat spaghetti night, isn't it?" I reminded her. The cook had this amazing spaghetti sauce recipe that no one could resist. On all-you-can-eat spaghetti night, the place was always packed to the rafters. "Maybe I can just order take out. Otherwise, I'd have to eat standing up."

"Good. Grab a seat at the bar," Joy suggested. "We'll get your favorite, then?"

"Yeah, sounds good."

I found a seat in the far corner of the restaurant's only bar. It was just inches away from the men's washroom. There were mostly guys sitting at the bar, many of them waiting to be seated for dinner. And for some reason, the men at the bar were always some of the most brazen in New York. I really was not in the mood to flirt or be propositioned. I tilted my body a little away from their direction and stared down on my cell phone.

"Oh, hi Kate!" chirped Diane, one of the servers who had worked there for over seven years. She was one of the few workers that I kept in touch with outside of work, as she was such a kind person. I reached up and gave her a quick hug.

"Hi, Diane how are you doing?" I asked. "Must be a hectic one for you."

"Yes, the usual for the spaghetti rush," she answered. "How are things with you?"

"Pretty good thanks," I replied.

"You should come back. Joy is a pain in the butt, and we miss you around here," Diane complained. "Her boyfriend's been giving her all sorts of trouble, and all she does is bring it to work. Between her parents, the boyfriend, and all those spa treatments and stylist appointments she's missing, I'm seriously tired of hearing all the billionaire drama."

"I can imagine," I answered. I knew it firsthand. Most people who've never been wealthy have this fairytale idea that the lives of the rich and famous are all glamour, excitement and easy. That couldn't be further from the truth. To me, it was all about control, manipulation, competition, and complicated relationships. In fact, I think that when Facebook created the 'it's complicated' relationship status, Mark Zuckerberg meant it for one of his snooty rich college buddies. Personally, I was much happier living a normal life as opposed to what I left behind.

"I think your food's ready dear," Diane said as she looked up from wiping the bar counter. "Let me go check."

She came back in a few moments with a brown bag and handed it over the counter to me. "Yup. It's all yours, Kate. Enjoy."

As I took the bag, Diane leaned close to me.

"Your parents phoned again. And they sent a PI here three days ago looking for you."

"Seriously?" I asked. "They will never give up, will they?"

"Maybe you should just call them and settle it once and for all," Diane suggested, speaking softly. "People change. Sometimes for the better. But if you never give them a chance, or give them forgiveness, you're taking peace away from your own life. You don't want to wait until there's something to regret, do you?"

I didn't answer. I just looked down at the bag. The last thing I wanted to do was talk about that.

+++

I walked home in a mental fog, resisting any and all attempts at eye contact from the people who passed by. I was used to the catcalls from men and the lingering, mean stares I got from women so often. Apparently I fit the traits of the man-stealing vixen. George would tell me all the time that not only did I have a phenomenal voice for radio, but that I was a stunner. Coming from anyone else, I would have considered it to be sexual harassment. But then again, it was George.

In any case, a lot of good it had done me to that point. Creepy guys ogling. Creepier guys cyber-stalking me on the radio station social media accounts. A jock boyfriend in high school who was more into admiring his reflection that even noticing I was around. A jerk boyfriend in college with not an ounce of romance in his DNA. And a sorry-ass, lying-through-his-teeth, smoking hot firefighter ex-boyfriend.

The lower Manhattan streets were always crowded, even at night. That night, however, seemed quieter than normal, and even I noticed it in my semi-distant state. I normally listen to music on my smart phone and would have had my headset on, but I didn't think to wear them that night. That's probably why the shrill scream of what sounded like a young girl or boy, caught my attention.

I'm not sure what got into me, perhaps it was my curiosity. I sped up my pace and walked towards the sound. I was in disbelief because the entire row of brownstone walk-ups on my street was going up in flames. People were spilling out of their units, seeming to grab as many things as they could. And at the end of the row, that's when I saw her. In the distance, the girl looked to be around 13, and was screaming up at a second-floor window, where a young boy was leaning out. It was my neighbor's kids that I used to see at the park opposite the restaurant from time to time.

"You have to jump!" she screamed.

"I'm scared. I can't," he answered weakly, coughing from the smoke escaping his room.

"You have to," she shouted at the top of her lungs.

"I can't."

It was so chaotic on the street that no one else noticed them. People were running in and out of their homes trying to grab what they could. The worry was probably intensified on people's faces because it was less than a year ago that the first two units of the row house had finally been repaired from the hurricane damage. Hadn't the street been through enough from the Frankenstorm?

I was on the only one whose attention was on those two kids. I had seen their parents frequently, taking them out on many evenings for dinner at the restaurant where I worked. They'd then cross the street and let the kids play in the small park across the road. Where in the hell were they?

I reacted on impulse, like instinct. The adrenaline must've taken over; my heart started pounding so hard in my chest. I ran to the end of the street because I remembered that a neighbor on the other end would leave his long-ass ladder on the side of the building. He had received several complaints from the other neighbors as it blocked the shortcut to the entrance of the E train.

All I remember was grabbing it, and pushing it onto the side of the walk-up stairway. I barely remember climbing up, grabbing the boy - who looked to be around six years old. I vaguely remember pulling him over my shoulder and climbing down the rungs of the ladder in what seemed like double steps. It was a blur, but when I got to the bottom, time seemed to completely slow down.

I was shocked at what I had done, and stood frozen in disbelief. It certainly had actually happened, because a crowd had gathered around the base of the ladder, and started to cheer and applaud in my direction. The boy seemed mostly fine, despite his soot-blackened clothes and skin. His sister held him tightly and was crying, probably in relief.

It was just about then, that truck No. 89 of the FDNY10 Station of Lower Manhattan made its way around the corner. Two police cruisers followed and the officers inside instantly began taking control. It was the police department's job to control the traffic as residents evacuated and attend to crowd control, while keeping the street clear for firefighters. And I knew that because we had done so many building-wide drills at the radio station after Hurricane Irene. The firefighters dismounted quickly and began to fight the blaze that was now threatening other homes in the next row of townhouses.

My muscles started aching, and it hit me then that I hadn't gone into my walk-up to grab anything from my place. I realize now it was the adrenaline fading and I started feeling weak, so I nearly collapsed on the edge of the sidewalk on the other side of the street. That's when a firefighter approached me.

"Ma'am," he said with authority and hero-like confidence. "I'm going to have to get you to stand all the way over there with the rest of your neighbors. We need to clear the street and get you all at least a block and a half away."

I looked up and all I remember was my arms going loose and my shoulder slumping forward.

When I came to I was on a stretcher, about to be put into the back of the ambulance vehicle. There was an oxygen mask over my nose and mouth, a brace around my neck, and a female paramedic leaning over me on my right side. I looked over to my left, and he was there. His left hand rested warmly but ever so gently on my shoulder. As weak and out of it as I was feeling, his touch sent chills and tingles throughout my body.

Hero Chemistry.

"Ma'am, this must be your purse," he said. "I'll make sure the paramedics take this with them so you have it once you get to the hospital."

I tried to speak but was weak and everything seemed blurry.

"You inhaled a lot of smoke when you jumped into the second-story bedroom to get him," he said. "That was really brave of you. Have you ever had firefighter training? Don't speak just nod yes or no."

I shook my head no, not realizing until then, that I had actually climbed into the window when I went up to get the child.

"Just stay still and we'll get you all taken care of."

They loaded me into the back of the ambulance, and it was a short ride to the hospital. And suddenly everything got blurry and started to fade away.

~~ Chapter Three ~~

I think I fell asleep or passed out again, because when I woke up, I was confused about my surroundings. I quickly realized I was in a shared recovery room. There was an IV in my left arm, connected to what looked like saline solution. It sounded like there was a lady in the hospital bed beside me, but I couldn't tell for certain because all of the curtains were drawn almost fully around me. All I could see was the doorway and a tiny picture frame beside it.

A doctor walked in and stood beside the bed, scanning the label of the hospital tag around my wrist with the tablet he had with him, to read the medical file they created for me.

"Good, you're awake," he said. "How are you feeling?"

"Fine, I think," I replied. "Just a bit weak."

"You suffered from moderate smoke inhalation, which is why you're probably weak. You have first degree burns on your forearms. We treated them and they're minor. You'll be coughing for some time, and that may weaken you further. But other than that, you're going to be ok."

"Well that's a relief, doctor," I responded softly.

"So this means we can release you in a few hours once you feel stronger," he continued. "Do you have anyone we can phone?"

I hesitated because I had no family in New York. "Um, I can probably call..."

George and Richard walked in just as I finishing my pathetic answer. George had a bunch of flowers and Richard, one of those silver helium-filled get well soon balloons. They stopped at the door when they realized the doctor was speaking to me.

"Come on in, gentlemen," the doctor said as he motioned them to enter and began to leave. "Miss Samuel. I'll check in on you in a few hours before the end of my shift."

"George, Richard. How did you find out I was here?"

"It was all over the news," George replied. "And we live two blocks away, remember? The smoke was everywhere. We came out right as we learned of it to look for you, but got to the street just as they were putting you into the back of the ambulance."

"Honey," said Richard. "Are you ok? You look like exhausted but in a much better state than we thought we'd find you. We were so worried for ya, girlfriend."

"I'm pretty fucked up, aren't I?" I replied. "I feel like crap."

I was so used to the guys swearing at the radio station that I'd become as potty-mouthed as they were, or maybe worse. Then I remembered another patient was in the bed beside me. "Oops."

"No you look surprisingly good," George chimed in. "Your row of brownstones is practically burned to the ground. They're calling you a hero. That was crazy what you did, but I'm so proud of you."

"How do you know what I did?" I questioned.

"One of your neighbors recorded it on their smartphone. It's been cycling on the TV and online news outlets for hours. And the clip has almost a million views on YouTube. You're practically a celebrity."

I smiled sheepishly for a moment, and then coughed uncontrollably for a few seconds. My throat and lungs burned still.

"Let me call the doctor," Richard said, his voice sounding full of worry.

"No, it's okay," I replied. "I'll be coughing for a while. I'm actually fine, and the doctor said they'll be releasing me pretty soon."

"Well that's good," said George. "The cough does sound pretty bad though."

I nodded.

"We'll wait here with you, and that way, once you get released we can take you home to our place."

"No, I'll just take a cab home," I answered, not wanting to inconvenience them, and really, all I wanted was a night's sleep in my own bed.

"Kate," Richard replied softly. "There is no home, remember? Your place is practically gone."

No home. That was the first time it hit me that the damage was real, and permanent.

"Oh, yeah," I said. "Um, I think I'll just stay in a hotel."

"You've gotta be kidding me Kate," George countered with an ever-so-stubborn stance. "We don't pay you enough to afford a New York hotel. You're staying with us, and that's final."

"So, what about all those other people who lived on the street? Are you letting them stay at your place too?"

"Stop being silly, woman," George said. "On the news, they said that most of those people had contents insurance and will be able to get reimbursed to stay at a hotel. But they have each other, and you just have us, remember?"

My parents were actually alive, and quite wealthy, living in Phoenix. However they disagreed with my choice of career, and gave me an ultimatum, as they were so used to doing anything they needed to, to control everyone around them. Business School or work in the family business. By then I had had enough. It wasn't enough that I was their daughter and had a passion for communications and media. I don't think I was ever enough to them.

So when I turned eighteen, I ran away with the savings I had accumulated over the years, which was a small fortune to some. It was enough to get me through college with just a part-time job. I never spoke to them again. They had always felt they could control everything and everyone with their money, including me. And I just didn't want to live that way. I didn't even think they knew where I lived, or whether was alive.

"True," I said. "Okay, I'll stay with you guys, but only for a few days, until I can find myself another place. There's no way I can..."

My room door opened, and it was the firefighter who was standing over me when I woke up in the stretcher. As he stood in the doorway, with the light from the hallway spilling from behind him into my dimly lit room, he looked glorious.

Standing there, he seemed much taller than I remembered. His short, dark blonde hair framed his clean-shaven, chiseled face. His muscled shoulders and broad chest were obvious, even under his entire fireman's uniform. He was breathtakingly handsome.

Hero.

"Sorry to interrupt you all," he began. "Miss Samuel, it seems that a couple of things fell out of your bag and were found on your street after the commotion died down. I just came to bring them back to you."

He produced my wallet which had all of my credit cards and ID, and my cell phone from his front pocket.

"And you are?" asked Richard, his eyes soaking in every inch of the firefighter's body with desire and delight. Sometimes Richard could be such an obvious pig. He was loyal to George but had a tendency to act in the most inappropriate way sometimes.

"Excuse me for not introducing myself. Lieutenant Lewis, of FDNY 10, Lower East Side station," he replied and turned back to me. "Ma'am, it's not procedure, however there's a lot of activity underway by Police and other city offices. Just trying to find temporary lodgings for the displaced families has taken some time because hotels are as capacity for some reason. So we all had to chip in to help out. Normally this would have been handed over to the police department, but they've been really occupied. And I thought you'd need this to get settled somewhere for the night."

"Thank you very much Lieutenant," I answered. "You're right. I'm not sure what I would do without these." I suddenly began to think about the things that were in my apartment and what of it might've been valuable, or held good memories. Other than my clothes and laptop, I couldn't think of anything. Everything else could have been replaced.

"Oh, it's no problem at all, ma'am," he replied. "I'll leave you to your friends now. What you did was remarkable. Very brave and selfless. My Fire Chief will probably be contacting you tomorrow to thank you personally. Would you mind writing out your temporary address where you'll be staying, telephone number, and email address for us?"

Temporary. Yet another reminder I was homeless. I looked up at George, who was already nodding for me to put their contact details down.

"Let me do it," insisted George. "She'll be staying with us."

I looked on silently as he took the paper and pen the Lieutenant provided, wrote down the address, and handed it back to him.

"Thank you. Well, have a good evening, ma'am," he said, then turned towards George and Richard. "Gentlemen." He seemed a little hesitant as he left, like he would have said more if George and Richard weren't there.

"Jesus Christ, that guy was so hot," Richard shouted after he left. "And in a firefighter's uniform of all things, George." He winked slyly at George.

George rolled his eyes. "Just can it, Rich," he said, with a tinge of jealousy. "Besides, it's really obvious that he has something for Kate. Kate, did you see the way he looked at you before he left? And he's got your number now! I'm putting down twenty bucks right now that he'll call you before the week is out. "

"Guys," I spoke up. "I have no energy right now. I think I'm just going to take a nap until they give the okay for me to leave. Why don't you guys just go home and when they're ready I'll take a cab to your place. "

"We already told you that we're going to stay," Richard countered. "Just have some rest, and we'll be out in the waiting room. And don't go dreaming about Mr. Hottie. He's hot like fire!"

It was a relief to have some time to myself. I was too tired to think, let alone interact. My mind wandered to Lieutenant Lewis. I wondered what his first name was. Right away, I caught myself. This is how it starts. I glamorize guys just like that without knowing who they are, and what they stand for. And then they rip my heart to shreds and kick it in the corner before they walk out the door. I was not going to let this happen again. And besides, what I really needed to worry about was what I was going to do to replace everything; where I was going to live; how things would get back to normal for me; and for all those people on my block.

I must've fallen asleep, because when I opened my eyes, the doctor was back in the room with his tablet, checking off some things with his stylus. There was a female nurse beside him as well.

"So Ms. Samuel," he started. "Everything is a go for you to leave now. The nurse here will remove your IV. You'll need to wear those bandages on your forearm for at least a few days. She'll give you some gauze and extra bandages to take with you."

"Thanks, Doctor," I replied quietly, still sleepy and foggy-headed, as the nurse began to remove the needle from my arm.

"Remember, you were exposed to the smoke for a while, so you may experience a few residual side effects. Symptoms like a lingering cough and hoarseness, chest pain, trouble breathing. Even eye irritation, headaches, abdominal pain or nausea. Those are normal and to be expected. But if you start to feel shortness of breath, faint at any time, or begin coughing up blood, that's not good, so for those symptoms, get to an urgent care clinic or back to the hospital right away. Okay?"

"Yes Doctor," I answered, somewhat concerned by the laundry list he rattled off.

"Someone will be right along with the wheelchair. Once the release papers are complete in a few minutes, they'll wheel you out to the entrance. And your friends are waiting outside so they're ready to take you home."

"Thanks."

"Oh, and there's also this envelope. Someone left it for you at the nurse's reception desk. I've got to go and check on some other patients, so take care of yourself. And great work today. What you did was something that most people would be too afraid to do. You saved that boy's life. He suffered from second- and third-degree burns, but he's alive and he'll be fine in time. I wanted to let you know that."

I nodded, because I didn't know what to say. After he and the nurse left, I looked down at the envelope with just my last name written on it. Inside it was a folded Post-it note. It read,

> *Ms. Samuel,*
> *Please contact FDNY 10 station at your earliest convenience.*
> *Lieut. Matt Lewis*
> *212 – 718 – 9999*

That was really weird, for him to leave a note like that for me. He had just taken my information, and already said that the Fire Chief would contact me. I couldn't figure it out, but also didn't have the intellectual adeptness to question it any further at that point. I decided I'd give them a call the next day.

George and Richard chatted like giddy schoolgirls the entire way home. Why? I'm not sure. I think they were always that way together. It probably didn't help that they had met the Lieutenant either. I wasn't able to focus much on what they said, and it was easy to tune them out for some reason. I think I just needed some rest. I had no clothes to change into when we got to their place, so George gave me a pair of his sweatpants and a T-shirt. I was so beat; I fell asleep in their guest room on the main floor right away.

~~ Chapter Four ~~

I slowly woke up in the sun-filled, warmly decorated room. It took a while to get up, but once I sat up I noticed a handwritten note on the dresser. It was from George, telling me that he had gone off to work and I could have the day off today so that I could rest. I looked over at the clock on the wall and saw that it was already after 1:00 P.M. I went out to the living room and plugged my iPhone into Richard's charger. Up until then I had still not turned on the television, listened to the radio, seen a newspaper, or logged onto any of the social media accounts on my phone.

As I'd been over to their place frequently, I was pretty comfortable with the layout and I knew where things were in the kitchen. I decided to make myself a coffee and try to chase away some of the fogginess. I hadn't eaten since the day before, so I was ravenous. I checked the fridge for some fruit or anything I could find, and turned on their kitchen TV.

I almost dropped the bowl of fruit yoghurt I had found when the reporter's coverage finally registered.

> *A local DJ is being hailed a hero today, after saving the life of a 9 year old boy. Twenty-two year old Kate Samuel sprang into action last night when a large fire broke out at a row of lower east side Manhattan townhouses. The young woman risked her life by climbing up a residential ladder to the boy's window, and even jumped in through the window when the scared child wouldn't come out to her.*

> *Amateur video captured by witnesses shows the woman climbing down the ladder with the boy in a fireman's carry over her shoulder.*

> *The boy suffered serious second- and third-degree burns to 20 percent of his body, but thanks to this quick-*

thinking young lady, doctors say he will have a full recovery. Miss Samuel suffered only minor injuries and was released from hospital last night. We have not been able to reach her for comment, quite understandable, given that Miss Samuel lived at one of the burned down townhomes.

Sadly, there appears to be two fatalities from the blaze; however Police and Fire officials have not released the names of the victims, whose bodies were seen being removed from Unit 16 this morning, after the fire was under control.

(Unit 16?)

FDNY 10 Station Fire Chief Bill Jameson released a statement today, thanking the woman for her bravery, calling it a "bold, courageous citizen's action", and will be recommending her for a Meritorious Service Award. The fire began in the middle of the row of homes, and the cause is still under investigation.

And the bad news does not seem to end there. Over 48 people in 18 families have been left homeless, as the fire is said to have caused extensive damage and will require the building to be demolished. Of the 18 families, seven reportedly did not have insurance. Incidentally, this street was also hit hard by Hurricane Irene back in late 2011, so we know it's a tough time for these families. City officials are working to find supports and locate temporary lodgings for these seven families.

In international news...

Temporary.

It was hard to believe what I was hearing. It was too much to sink in. My knees weakened on learning there were fatalities. I took the coffee to try and perk up, and went over to the living room sofa to sit. Disbelief. I barely remember doing all of that, and to hear her calling me a hero was an even bigger surprise. I did what anyone else probably would have done. I mean, was I supposed to leave the little boy there? I just did what had to be done. And people were dead? I wracked my brain trying to think of who was missing last night. Who lived at Unit 16? I knew most of the neighbors, maybe not by name, but I'd seen their faces and greeted them whenever we saw each other as we went about our routines. I couldn't think straight.

I got up and walked over to turn on my phone, which was on Richard's charger. That was the moment when I think it started to sink in. There was a constant, almost never-ending sequence of buzzing, beeping, and pinging as the text messages, voicemail, and Facebook alerts loaded onto the phone. I didn't know what to check first, so I looked at my text messages. There were over 60 from a variety of phone numbers, and the majority of them were from TV and news stations asking me to contact them for an interview.

Text messages just kept loading and loading, row after row of messages appearing. After the tenth message, I pressed the home button. I logged on to Facebook and it was like my news feed and alerts just blew up. Congratulatory messages in my inbox from friends and people I didn't know, comments in the news feed, and I was tagged in hundreds of the same pictures of me, descending the ladder. Images of me on the ladder, images of me, carrying the boy on my shoulder, even one of me in the stretcher, with the lieutenant and paramedic standing over me. I couldn't look at it all. I couldn't digest it all in one bite. I decided not to check my voice messages, and as soon as I put the phone down, it rang. I recognized the number was George's at the station, so I answered.

"Hello?"

"Are you getting it now Kate?' he asked, with such excitement in his voice. "You're a celebrity!"

"My phone is full of messages from people I don't know, George. And journalists. And I just turned on the news. Uh, I just, it just doesn't feel real," I tried to change the subject. "How is everything where you are? Did you get someone to fill my timeslot?"

"Yes never mind about that," he answered. "We've got it all under control. If you're up for it, you can come in tomorrow. Just a little word of warning. You're going to be a bit surprised when you get here."

"Why?" I didn't like the sound of that.

"You'll see," George said, with a hint of glee in his voice. "Did you call back the FDNY guy?"

"No, I'm just waking up. I'll give them a call as soon as I can clear my head."

"They phoned a couple times. I gave them your cell number, and our address too. Don't be surprised if Lieutenant Lewis pays a visit."

"What? What do they want?"

"I really don't know. Probably all that talk about giving you a commendation. Okay, well get some rest, and I'll see you in a few hours. Dean has got the evening shift tonight. "

"Alright. Talk to you later. And George, I didn't get to thank you and Richard last night for putting me up here with you, and staying with me at the hospital. It means a lot to me that you guys have been there for me all this time. And I..."

"Not to worry, Kate. It's no problem at all. Look I've got to take care of something, but I will see you later. Take care okay? Bye."

I turned the phone off as I hung up as I couldn't handle the buzzing of new messages, and didn't want to take any more calls. I needed time to take it all in. However, it didn't seem like time was a commodity I had anymore, because right there and then, the door knocked.

I looked through the peephole, and it was Lieutenant Lewis. What was he doing here? I kept the security chain on the door and just open it a crack, just enough to make eye contact.

"Hello? What can I do for you Lieutenant?"

"Hello ma'am. I'm here on behalf of Fire Chief Bill Jamieson FDNY 10 station. We tried to contact you a few times, so the chief asked me to come down here to inform you that he's put your name in for a citizen's commendation. Congratulations ma'am."

"You can call me Kate," I answered. "And this is how it normally happens? I thought that these kinds of things would happen in a letter or something more formal."

"Well, no. Ma'am, uh, Kate. Normally it would be more formal. However, the award service is in two days, and the mayor insisted that we add you to this upcoming ceremony. So with that decision, there wouldn't be enough time to get an announcement and invitation to you by mail. I have the letter and invitation here though."

"Oh, I see," I replied. "Um, hold on, let me open the door." He was in a plain white shirt and black dress pants this time, as though he had just come out of a business meeting. His muscled shoulders and chest pressed through his crisp shirt, and broad toned legs strained the seams of his tailored pants. He was breathtakingly handsome. A part of me was completely overtaken by his dominant presence. He looked so strong, so sexy.

Hero.

It was not the time or place, but I had to resist imagining him running his hand through my hair, ripping my clothes off, and us having an uncontrollable moment of passion together. Sure, it was not the time or place, but I was already wet for him. I put every effort into getting all of it out of my mind as he walked in through the door.

"This is the invitation Kate," he said, not moving any further than a couple steps away from the door. As I reached my hand out for it, our fingers brushed together and our eyes locked. Electricity charged through my fingers, feeling like there was some invisible chemistry emanating from him to me. Like a primal, prehistoric force. I turned my head slightly and gulped a little too loudly. There was sadness in his eyes.

"Thank you Lieutenant Lewis. It's still a big blur for me right now. Once everything calms down I'll definitely make every attempt to come."

"Not to worry, the media hype will pass soon enough," he said, then re-focused on the invite. "The invitation allows for two guests, which can be your parents or anyone else that you'd like to have with you."

"Oh," I said in hesitation. I didn't want to have to get into explaining why my parents would not be there. "My parents live out of town. It's probably not enough notice. Can I bring George and Richard?"

"Definitely," he answered. "Anyone you want."

"Great. Well, would you like tea or something to drink?"

Hero defenses dropping.

"No ma'am," he replied quickly. "Well, yes I would, but I'm actually late for a meeting. Another time, maybe?"

"S-Sure," I stuttered, partly relieved, but also a little disappointed. "Definitely. No problem at all. Thank you for coming by."

"No, problem ma'am," he said. "Looking forward to seeing you at the ceremony. Actually can I ask you something?"

"Sure."

"I saw the replays of your rescue and the way you held the boy was remarkable."

"Thanks," I said.

"Have you had firefighter training? You used the fireman's hold."

"No, I just grew up on a cattle farm. That's how I learned to carry the smaller calves we had. It was nothing, really."

"Really?" he answered. "Where?"

"Just outside Phoenix," I replied.

"Nice," he said. He seemed to want to talk more, but stopped himself.

"Well, enjoy the rest of your afternoon, Kate."

As he left, I felt torn. I could have turned on my flirtatious side and may have turned that into a date if I wanted. I was just not myself, and really didn't have the inclination to be 'the vixen'. In the end, I was always the one to get hurt. Especially with these hero-types. I pushed the door closed and locked it.

~~ Chapter Five~~

No sooner after sitting back down in the living room, the doorbell rang again. Thinking it was the Lieutenant, I just unlocked the door and opened it without checking through the peephole. Big mistake. I was met with over ten news reporters, cameras, voice recorders, microphones and blinding camera lights. They talked over each other, asking undiscernible questions that all merged into one loud and hounding sound. One female reporter waved her hand at the others, and they quieted down so that I could hear her question.

"Miss Samuel, how are you feeling now that you're being hailed as a heroine?"

"I don't know," I answered. "Better now."

"What were you thinking when you took the ladder and climbed up to save the boy?"

"I just did what anyone else would do," I said, trying to be calm.

"Did you know him?"

"Did I know who?" I asked.

"The child you saved."

"Well," I began. "I've seen him and his family playing in the park form time to time, but no."

"What do you feel about your other displaced neighbors who are...,"

I suddenly caught myself and started to take control of the situation, before things got too intense.

"Ladies and gentlemen," I started, "as you can tell, I'm standing in the doorway with just my robe on. I am still recovering from my injuries. I am very saddened by the tragedy of last night's fire. I feel I did what I needed to do to help. I lost my home too. I'd be happy to give a more detailed statement or interview once I've recovered from my injuries. Thank you all for your support. Sorry, I have no further comment at this time."

I turned away from all of the microphones, overwhelmed, and quickly stepped inside and locked the door. I could still hear them, shouting questions through the door, and reporting back to their respective station listeners from right outside.

How did they know I was here?

I walked over to the kitchen and it seemed to quiet down after about five minutes. But then the door knocked again. Why would they harass me at a time like this? I began to understand what celebrities felt on a day-to-day basis. This time, I opened the door again, impatient and ready to give them a piece of my mind.

"What the hell do you people want from m-?" I asked before fully opening the door, then realizing that it was the Lieutenant again. "Oh, Lieutenant, I'm sorry. There was just a bunch in media reporters and cameras at my door, and I don't know how they had this address."

"Are you all right?" he asked.

"Yes, I'm fine," I answered.

"I think they may have followed me here," he said, a little embarrassed. "When I got back to the car two blocks away, I noticed them all entering your building. I'm late for a meeting, but I thought you could probably use a little help. Glad you were able to send them packing."

"Oh, so I have you to thank for this, Lieutenant?" I joked, smiling.

"I am really sorry," he added. "I should've known they'd be tailing me because a few of them were down at the station, grilling everyone to find out more about you. And by the way, call me Matt."

"It's all right," I tried to reassure him. "I know my way around the PR block. So you came back just to help me?"

"I just thought that in your state, you might need a little help," he admitted.

"Well, that was really kind of you," I said. "I appreciate that. Here, let me get you some tea. It's cold out, and you're late anyway, so it's the least I can do to make up for it." I started walking towards the kitchen, figuring this time he'd say yes.

"Okay," he conceded. "Sure, thanks Kate."

As I turned to grab the teapot at the kitchen island counter, the room started spinning, and my vision blurred. I had to hold on to stop myself from falling. He must have noticed I was on weak footing, because the next thing I knew, I felt his arms around my waist, holding me up against his solid, muscular chest, to keep me from falling. My body was weak, and he instinctively stretched out one arm behind my knees, picked me up with ease, and began to carry me over to the living room sofa. His body was so warm and solid. I leaned into his strong arms and rested my head against his neck. The smell of his cologne was irresistible and therapeutic.

Hero.

He lowered me gently on the sofa and reached for the blanket draped over George's favorite lazy boy chair.

"Sorry," I said slowly. "I must still be a little dizzy. I'm sure I'll be fine."

"No," he answered with a commanding, protective tone. "Don't move. I'll get you some tea."

"He walked over to the kitchen put the kettle on. He comfortably maneuvered his way around, searching the cupboards to find the teabags and a teacup for me. As the kettle was heating up, he reached for his cell phone in his pocket and sent a text message.

"I just sent a message ahead that I'll have to miss this meeting that I'm late for," he said. "Not to worry. My vice president James will help, and I'll get up to speed later."

"Vice president?" I asked. "That's an unusual title for the fire service."

"Yes, not there," he answered. "It's not for my day job. It's for my family's company. I still sit on the board as chairman."

"Yeah?" I asked weakly, thinking I would have to ask him what company his family owned when I felt a little better.

"Not to worry about that right now," he countered, as he walked towards me with the tea. "It's not a big deal. James will take care of it. And I'll stay and take care of you until your friends get here."

My heart melted. "You don't have to do that," I resisted. "I'll be fine, really."

"I am staying," he announced. "Besides, I feel bad that I didn't catch you quickly enough as you passed out on the sidewalk yesterday. I told the paramedics to check you out for a concussion, and they said you were fine. So it must just be the smoke inhalation that has you feeling dizzy."

"Oh, that's okay," I replied. "Okay, fine. Stay. Thank you."

"What room are you staying in?" he asked. "I'll grab your pillow."

I raised my forearm slowly and pointed to the guest room. He disappeared around the corner and then came back with two pillows and the comforter from the bed.

"Here." He propped my head up with the two pillows then spread the comforter out and covered me gently. Our eyes met as he leaned over to tuck the comforter behind my shoulders. I was at a loss for words and I hoped my eyes wouldn't betray my thoughts. God, he was handsome; strong, and so thoughtful to take care of me that way. He was so physically appealing, that I could feel my nipples hardening in response to his body being so close to mine. His warmth emanated from him to every fiber of my being in this primal, carnal and mesmerizing wave.

Control yourself Kate.

As he stood up, I looked shyly at his body. He had broad shoulders. And those strong arms had held me so protectively. I remembered the warmth of his rock hard chest. There was a lot to appreciate about him.

He sat in George's chair and watched me intently, never turning his attention to anyone or anything else. I closed my eyes, aroused but tired and barely able to stay awake. I felt safe.

+++

When I woke up, I had forgotten where I was, and was confused for a few moments. It was already dark, but that meant little as it was already late November and got dark well before the dinner hour. I realized I was in George's guest bedroom, under the same comforter that Matt had gently wrapped me in. I pressed my nose into it and closed my eyes as I smelled the faint scent of his cologne. I could hear George and Richard in the living room or kitchen. They were bantering as they usually did. It was a familiar sound, hearing them cooking dinner and play-arguing over the usual fashion, celebrity news, and other trivial topics. Slowly, my recollection came back. I had fallen asleep in the living room, so Matt must have carried me to place me in the bed. I didn't remember anything else.

I sat up slowly to get my bearings, and Richard must have heard me.

"Get your ass back into bed, Missy," he shouted from the living room, as he walked towards my door. "You need to rest, Miss Famous."

Miss Famous. More like my 15 minutes.

"Where's Matt?" I asked, peering around Richard, into the living room to see if he was still there, silently hoping that he was.

"He stayed until we got here," Richard answered. "He actually just left about a half an hour ago. He explained everything, and we saw the reporters hounding you. You handled your fine self like an ace on TV. You whipped those fucking reporters into shape, sistah, and you did it with style and poise."

"Richard is right," George chimed in at the door. "You're a natural, and you handled yourself really well. The public is in love with you. And everyone wants to know more. We've had about 200 calls for you at the station. People are calling to say they are so proud of you. Reporters are trying to get exclusive interviews. And get this. You got a call from the Mayor of New York City. Do you freaking understand what that means? For you? For the station? Great job, Kate. But next time, put some clothes on and do your hair before you answer the door. You looked like hell. Cute and adorable as a button, but like hell."

I smiled, but nothing was registering fully. I was still thinking about Matt. Why did he stay there with me? Why did he give up his important meeting to take care of me? And who was he really? I wondered about him and his family and his business, making a mental note to Google him, once I felt better.

"That was nice of him," I said.

"Who? Matt?" said Richard. As I nodded he exclaimed, "Girl, you are batting 100! All this media attention, you saved that boy, and now it looks like your knight in shining armor is here to rescue you and rock your world. If I had a few hours alone with that guy, well I just don't know, I..."

"Let her eat and get some rest, Richard," George said firmly. "It's late, and she doesn't need your rapid fire, down in the gutter, conversation. Besides, we need her at the station bright and early tomorrow, remember?"

"What for?" I jumped in.

"You'll see," he said, smiling mysteriously. "Now get back into bed and let me grab the dinner tray so you can have some food in you before you go back to sleep."

They left me alone as I pecked at the bread, bowl of soup, and grilled chicken salad they brought me. I didn't have an appetite but knew that I should eat something. All I could think about was Matt. Was I overreacting about what he did for me? He did say that he felt responsible for leading the reporters to George and Richard's place, so that should have explained why he felt obligated. That, and the fact that he let me hit my head when I passed out on the sidewalk. Not that it was his fault at all, but it did explain why he would stay. It was just over twenty- four hours since the fire, and I'd seen Matt four times. He was slowly weaving his way into my psyche.

After getting ready for bed, I lay down but couldn't sleep. He was on my mind. I drifted into a restless sleep with visions of the fire, the little boy and his sister, and Matt holding me in his arms, looking deeply into my eyes like he wanted to tell me everything.

~~ Chapter Six ~~

"Wake up, Sunshine!" Richard shouted from my bedroom door. I was already awake, but still thinking about how surreal the last couple of days were. I was also planning out some things I'd need to be ready to say when I got back to work, and if the reporters happened to be there or on my way in.

"George wants me to make sure that you get in on time," Richard said as he walked in. "He left really early to be prepared for your surprise today."

"What surprise?" I asked, knowing that Richard would not budge, but still taking a chance that he might give me a hint, all things considered.

"Uh-uh, missy," he said as he shook his head with his eyes closed. "The vault is shut. Get dressed and get your butt into work and you'll find out soon enough." He reached over and pulled my arms to help me out of bed.

"Okay, I'll be ready in twenty minutes," I said, but remember that I had no clothes to wear. "Richard, I will need to borrow a shirt and some pants from you guys. I don't have anything anymore." And that's when I broke down. I was never the materialistic type of person, but suddenly I felt the loss. There was nothing left of anything that may have meant anything to me. My body shook and crying turned to weeping, and overtook me fully.

Richard put a protective arm over my shoulder and sat silently beside me on the edge of the bed. Once I started to calm down, he left the room and came back in a few minutes with a pink men's shirt, and blue jeans. "I called George, and reminded him that you need to stop to do a little bit of shopping before you get in. We're so sorry that we completely forgot about that. He's asked that you tried to come in by eleven AM. I've gone a little bit of time so why don't we go together? You know I rock at all things fashion, and you can use a bit of company. Deal?"

"Sure. Thanks Richard," I answered softly, still red-faced and catching my breath.

I showered and got dressed in Richard's stylish clothes, which actually didn't look too bad on me. I had a bit of breakfast, and then we decided to walk to a few of the nearby boutiques that open a little earlier than normal. Richard had all the details on where to find a good fashion bargain, and the best quality possible. On the way there, Richard found a way to make me smile. He was good at that.

Richard was like a five-year-old stuck in a grown man's body. He would climb onto the street-side park benches and sing out loud with his air microphone. He even ran through sprinklers that were on at full power on one street. He was completely drenched by the time we got to the first boutique. I loved seeing that side of him. He really was a beautiful soul, full of laughter, energy, fascination for the banal. And I was all the more inspired, considering what he lived through a few years ago.

After all that searching through several boutiques, I decided on staying in what I was wearing. Richard didn't mind too much because he bought some things to change out of his wet clothes. I smiled as I entered the radio station main entrance, wondering how often that actually happened to him.

As I got off the elevator onto our floor, no one was around. All the cubicles and sound engineer stations were empty. I put my bag down and walked towards the set where we did our live radio shows.

All eight of the day staff were cramped in the radio room with a large sign behind them that read 'Congratulations Kate'. I walked in with a smile, however was still not in that festive type of mood to celebrate. They queued up the DJ on shift, and he announced a lofty welcome back to the room and to all our listeners. After much applause and hugs and pats on my back, the group dispersed to their respective workstations, and George asked me to come sit with him in the small outer office.

"So, how are you feeling?" he started.

"I think I'm mostly back to normal," I answered, trying to have a little more excitement in my voice. "Thanks so much for the warm welcome back. You really didn't have to."

"Oh, there's so much more," he continued. "Guess who's going to be here at noon, going live on the air at our station, because of you?"

"Who?" I asked, figuring it would be the station owner, or some delegate from the police or fire Department.

"The mayor of New York City!" he said aloud.

"What? Why? For me?" I asked.

"Who else?" he said with sarcasm. "Of course, for you. He wanted to give you a special thanks in person, and also liked the idea of doing it live from our building as a public address. I believe they're going to leverage the media to make an announcement about the displaced homeowners from the fire, yourself included, remember?"

"Well it's a good thing that it's the radio, because look at what I'm wearing," I answered. "Richard found more at the boutiques that I did. So I'm still wearing his clothes from this morning."

"Hold that thought," he said. "The media's going to be in a frenzy outside. And as it's a public event, there's probably going to be a lot of people showing up as well. "

"I wish I would've known before," I answered. "Why was this supposed to be such a surprise?"

"Um because, the station manager is going to offer you a promotion," he answered. "But don't let him know that I gave you the heads up."

"George, it's a lot to take, don't you think?" I said with a heavy sigh at the end. "I have no place to live, I have no clothes, everything that may have meant something to me in that apartment is now gone. And here I am getting ready to accept a commendation and a promotion, when I haven't even come to terms with everything that's happened."

"Just get through today," he tried to reassure me. "A day at a time, okay honey? Everything is going to be fine. And you're one of the lucky ones, remember? You had an insurance policy, right?"

"Yes I did, but I still feel the loss."

"Try to focus on the next hour," he offered as consolation. "Why don't you go check with Annie to see if she has any extra clothes she can lend you? You two are the same size, right? Now go take care of that and be back here at a quarter to noon."

I was not in the mood to go asking Annie or anyone else to borrow their clothes, but George walked me over and did the asking. And she was very willing and helpful, taking me to a small locker room and showing me the three spare outfits she had. She was around my size, but I stood at least half a foot taller than her, so none of her pants fit me. She did find a black, below-the-knee pencil skirt that more or less fit me. And I opted for her white dress shirt and pink button-down sweater that were definitely too short, but looked okay when I pushed the sleeves up to my elbow.

I have nothing and am homeless.

I knew the pity party in my brain would eventually end, but at that time, it was all I could think of.

+++

I got to the main entrance of our building just a few minutes before noon. I realized then that George may have understated the event that was to come. Hundreds of people had already gathered outside and had spilled into the street. There were police officers redirecting traffic and beginning to control the crowd with wooden barriers. Some members of the public held framed photographs of a couple. I couldn't make out who they were. Looking back, perhaps I was in denial.

At one side of the stairs was a group of first responders who had plunged in to fight the inferno which erupted that night. Every so often, the crowd would turn toward them and give a round of applause. Piling up on the right side was every type of local and regional media outlet – radio, TV, newspaper, online outlets, magazines, the works. A podium and microphone was positioned at the top of the stairs. Several media outlets had clipped and secured their branded mics to the podium for better sound quality during the address. George was near it, looking around to the building as though he was waiting for someone to come out.

Within minutes, a black town car slowly came through the parting crowd. The Mayor stepped out, and was quickly flanked by two security guards. He shook hands with a few onlookers, making his way up the stairs to the podium. He leaned in and greeted George and they exchanged a few words then looked back at the building entrance again. Then George walked inside and called out to me.

"Come on, Kate," he said. "They're waiting for you."

As we walked through the entrance, a booming round of applause erupted from the crowd. They were cheering for me? I wasn't prepared for that. In the blur of it I made out the Lieutenant with his firefighter colleagues. He nodded at me and smiled as though to say, "break a leg". The Mayor raised his right arm to get the attention of the crowd, and then began his speech.

"Citizens of New York City, we are here to take a moment to remember, to recognize, to begin healing and to rebuild. The fire at 6th Avenue was a tragedy. We want to remember that it displaced families, caused tens of millions of dollars in damage, and sadly, an almost unbearable loss of two people who perished during this local disaster. No passage of time can erase the lives lost, the injured and the damage caused by this tragedy from our consciousness. I know for some of us it feels like the wound has been reopened. It's been a difficult few years and this is why we will continue to rally together as a community.

"We also want to recognize the bravery and committed service of the firefighters of FDNY 10 station. These men and women risked their lives every day to save our precious loved ones. And it's their job. But if it weren't for the quick thinking and courage of Miss Kate Samuel, there may have been one more that burden for our community to bear. The city of New York extends its thanks to you.

"And we want to begin to heal and to rebuild. As a community, our residents are resilient, determined, and have extraordinary kind of character. This is what we need to hold on to as we move forward. I pray, and I will continue to pray, that we will continue to rally together and support each other until we all returned to some sense of normalcy. And once we rebuild, we will be that much stronger.

"Within each and every one of us is the capacity to lift ourselves up, in dignity and in strength. Yes, there will be here, and great suffering for the loss of Mr. and Mrs. Holstein, who lost their lives during the fire. But we will show great generosity and support to their surviving children, and..."

Mr. and Mrs. Holstein? It couldn't be. Those were the parents of the two children from that night. Their names came flooding back as I had handled their credit cards at the restaurant a few times before.

That is all that I remembered from the Mayor's speech. I felt my head spinning and knees weakening, and at the last moment, reached my arm over to George's shoulder, just before bracing myself for the fall. I didn't quite make it to the ground, because I felt strong arms hold me up before I passed out.

Hero.

~~ Chapter Seven ~~

I woke up in a hospital bed a few hours later. As I opened my eyes and looked around, Lieutenant Lewis was sitting in the chair beside me.

"What happened?" I began to ask. "And why are you here?"

"You fainted," he replied, then started with a smile. "Luckily I was there to catch you this time. The paramedics were there for the ceremony, so they were able to get you here pretty quickly. I think you may have a concussion, but the doctor will be here to discuss that with you."

"So why did *you* stay with me?" I couldn't resist asking. "Where's Richard or George?"

"They were both very busy so I offered to stay," he answered, then joked, "Just accept it; you're irresistible when you're unconscious."

"Funny guy," I smiled. It seemed like fate wanted to keep Matt and I connected, and he was not resisting it either. "So what happened after I passed out? At the ceremony, I mean."

"Well, the mayor only had a few more words left in his speech when you fainted," he started. "Sorry to say this, but it did cause quite a stir."

"How do you mean?" I probed, though a part of me just wanted to keep the conversation going.

"Well," he answered, "All eyes were already on you, in admiration, so it was a distraction. I wouldn't worry about it though. People understand what you've been through. And it may have saved you from the rush of journalists who have been waiting to get a piece of you."

All of a sudden the memory of what the Mayor had said flooded back to me. It was those kids' parents who died in the fire. I felt like all of the blood drained out of my head, and my heart sank.

"Are you all right?" he asked. "What's wrong?"

"Those people that died," I replied. "I didn't realize that it was actually them. Could I have saved them somehow? Everything happened so fast, I..."

"Listen, Kate," Matt said with a firm yet gentle tone. He leaned forward, looking into my eyes and putting his hand on my forearm, squeezing gently to get his point across. "It was not your fault. You saved their son. There was nothing else you could have done in the short time that we all had. You saved their son and I know they would be so relieved to know that he has his whole life ahead of him, because of you."

I wanted to reply, but I didn't have any words. We just looked at each other. The moment was too intense. There was a primal magnetism between us, and there was almost no resisting it, until it was unbearably uncomfortable. I turned my head and closed my eyes, confused.

"There's something I should tell you Kate," Matt started. "I think you should know that..."

Matt's voice trailed off as the doctor walked in.

"So, young lady," he started. "You don't have a concussion, but you're still suffering from the aftereffects of the smoke inhalation. I'm going to release you now, but you need to take it easy for at least two to three days. Understood?"

"Yes, Doctor," I answered.

"It's great to help nurse a hero back to health," he joked, "but I don't want to see you in the emergency room again."

As he walked off, Matt said quietly to me, "I'm going to make sure that you follow his advice, except for the award ceremony tomorrow. The chief would give me hell if you don't show up, and that's because the Mayor would give him hell. I'll wait outside while you get dressed. I'll take you home. "

+++

When we left the hospital, it was just after five PM. Matt supported my arm firmly, holding most of my body weight, as he was so strong. As we walked outside, he took me to his car, which was one of the top Maserati models and I don't think I had seen one like it for a while. Not since I left.

"Nice car," I said as he opened the passenger door and helped me in.

"Yeah, thanks," he answered. "This one's my favorite."

He walked around to the driver's side and got in quickly, then asked, "Are you hungry? We should get you something to eat."

"I'd love to," I said. "But I'm sure Richard or George will make me something when I get home."

"Come on," he persisted. "I could use the company. Besides, you won't say no once you know where I'd like to take you for dinner."

"Why not?" I asked.

"Because I'd like to take you to my favorite restaurant," he offered. "It's a quaint little traditional Italian family restaurant called Sabatini's."

"No," I said in disbelief. "Not the Sabatini's at Fifth and Main? That's where I worked for at least a year."

"So that explains it!" he answered with enthusiasm. "That's why you're so familiar. I thought I knew you from somewhere else, possibly through a family friend. But now I realize that's where I've seen you before."

"But I would've remembered you too," I said. "How come I don't remember you?"

"Well," he started. "That place is so busy, I'm surprised if you remember any of your customers. I go in there every Friday, like clockwork. And sometimes I pop in for takeout."

"That's why I never saw you, I guess," I answered. "I was off Fridays. Okay, sure, I don't mind stopping there for dinner before you take me home."

It was a short drive there, and Matt was such a gentleman. He insisted on coming around to my side and helping me out of the car as I stood up. He held me firmly around my shoulder, protecting me to ensure I was supported as we walked. I leaned gently on him as we strolled in, feeling safe. As we entered the restaurant, several of the hostesses and waiters rushed over to hug and congratulate me for saving the Holstein boy. They greeted Matt politely as several of them seemed to know him. We were seated at what he said was his usual table.

"So how are you feeling?" Matt asked. "Any dizziness?"

"No, I'm good thanks," I answered. "I'm famished, actually. Thanks for insisting on coming here."

"That's great," he replied. "See? Matt knows best. And do you know what you want to order?"

"I think so," I said. "One thing's for sure. The chef makes a mean cannelloni formaggio on the à la carte menu. What's your favorite dish?"

"Cannelloni formaggio," he said with a smile. "I order it almost every time I come here. It's settled, then." He called the server over and ordered for both of us, and added a bottle of expensive red wine, possibly the only one that the restaurant carried. And it made sense, because I vaguely remembered having to work on Friday night to cover one of the other staff. And I had served this same brand of wine to a well-dressed gentleman who sat in this part of the restaurant.

"I think I remember now," I said. "I mean I remember you. But you were so quiet. So reserved. You seemed like a completely different person."

"Yes," he answered, and I could see his face sadden. "That was around the time that my father passed away. It was a tough time because he was a wonderful dad."

"Oh," I hesitated. "I'm so sorry." I didn't know what to say.

"No, don't be," he answered. "There's no way you could have known. And it's all right. I had lost my mom just a month before that. It was hard. Really hard. But I'm done my grieving and I'm fine now." He paused for a moment, thinking. "And what about you? Do you still have your parents?"

I hesitated, then answered, "It's complicated."

"And what does that mean?" he asked, as he poured us both some of the wine they brought over.

"I'm still not comfortable talking about it," I answered, then thought how selfish I was being, given what he just shared. "Yes, they're still alive. We had a falling out almost 5 years ago and I ran away just before my freshman year at college. It was always about control with them. They thought their money could buy anything and anyone, including their own daughter.

"I'm sorry you're estranged from them," he said softly. "You know, time does have a way of making us put things in perspective. Maybe they've realized how much they lost and have changed?"

"I don't think they have the capacity to change," I said bluntly. I noticed a disappointed and sad look on his face, and then softened my tone. "I'm sure anything is possible, but I am not holding my hopes up. Where Mr. and Mrs. Samuel are concerned."

"So what if you parents were here in New York?" he asked intently. "What if they were at the press conference? What would you do then?"

"I doubt they could be anywhere and keep a low profile," I stated. "Everyone would know, and they'd make a point of making it all about them." I didn't want to think about them, let alone have a conversation on their likely behaviors. "Sorry Matt, can we change the subject?"

"Sure," he said, looking away.

"So what were you going to tell me in the hospital," I questioned.

"What?" he asked, his mind clearly distant.

"You were about to tell me something when the doctor walked in," I reminded him.

Just then, the server brought over our dinner. He looked relieved for this distraction from my question, so I knew I had to persist to get him to tell me. Admittedly, it might have all just been in my head.

"So what was it?" I pressed him. I needed to know.

"It was nothing," he answered. "No big deal. I just wanted to let you know that when you fainted, no one went back to your office to get your purse."

"Oh," I answered. "I'm definitely getting used to having no worldly possessions. So what's another loss?"

"Well, you have me," he said with a broad smile.

Somehow, that didn't help at that moment. I was quiet for the first few bites of dinner, and then he did his best to loosen me up. He started talking about what to expect the next night at the ceremony. He joked about some of the formalities and that made me relax as well. And I think I was on my second glass of wine as we started eating, so I was beginning to warm up. He joked and we laughed throughout dinner. He was very easy-going. I was enjoying his company, probably more than I should have.

"Okay, Miss Kate Samuel," he announced. "It's time I take you home."

Within a few minutes of leaving the restaurant, we were parked in front of George's house. It was a good thing that he took me to the door. I didn't have any keys, or my phone for that matter. And George and Richard weren't at home. Matt phoned their cell, but there was no answer. We waited in his car a few minutes, chatting as he kept joking to make me comfortable.

"It's getting late," Matt said. "We can't have you waiting out in the cold when you should be resting like the doctor said. I have a lot of room at my place and you can sleep there tonight. It beats waiting around for your friends to come back, and you really need your rest. Is that okay? I promise I'll be a gentleman."

It may have been the wine or his being such good company because I simply said, "Okay sure." After all, I didn't have another option, and I was genuinely tired.

We got to his building fairly quickly. He lived just about 15 blocks away from my old place.

Homeless.

He stopped, helped me out of the car, and handed his keys to the valet at his condo building. We walked up the red carpet of a luxurious entrance to his building, and the concierge greeted him by name. He instinctively pressed the button to call down the next elevator for him. We went up to what I think was the 20th floor and when we exited the elevator there was no lobby. He must have owned the entire floor because the elevator opened onto an all marble entryway.

And what an impressive condo apartment it was. The expansive hallway was elegantly decorated in light colors and light grey granite flooring. As we walked in, there were large matching mosaics on the walls and the rooms on each side had gigantic rugs laid between elegant pieces of furniture. Straight ahead, about 40 feet away from the elevators were double staircases leading up two flights of stairs. We walked past the stairwell and beyond it another 40 or so feet were large floor-to-ceiling glass windows. They offered an outstanding view of the city. It was breathtaking just standing there. Outside was a large balcony and with a few well-manicured shrubs, sleek silver dome-shaped globe lights and classy deck furniture.

"Wow, nice place," I said quietly. In a way, it reminded me of my parents' condo in Boston. I really didn't want to think about them and spoil my good mood, made better by the wine, great conversation and the refreshing laughs I had enjoyed earlier with Matt.

"Thanks," he replied. "My mother decorated it before she passed and I never could bring myself to redo it to my taste. Well, let me show you your room. You must be exhausted by now."

He led me by the hand, and as he walked me up the stairwell to the second floor, I couldn't help but feel completely attracted to him. He took me to a spacious room with a massive king-sized four poster bed, decorated in marigold and tan. It was enormous, but also cozy and welcoming.

"There're some clothes in the closet that should fit you," he continued. "It all belongs to my younger sister Sara. She's at college in UCLA but stays with me whenever she's in town."

"Thanks Matt," I answered. "I can use a set of pajamas and maybe something to wear tomorrow night."

"Feel free to use anything you want," he added. "Anything at all." He put his hand on my shoulder and squeezed gently. His touch was so warm, so inviting. I tilted my head and he cupped one side of my face with his hand. I closed my eye for a moment. It was just good to feel his touch.

"Alright," he said as he released my cheek. "I'll let you settle in and get to bed. If you need anything, I'm just three doors down on the left. Night Kate."

"Night Matt," I started.

As he walked through to the door, I called out to him. "Matt, I just want to say thanks. I'll call George again tomorrow morning and make arrangements to go back there during the day."

"No need to worry about that now," he replied. "Everything will get sorted out. Sleep well."

As he left, I sat on one side of the bed and took my shoes off. I couldn't help thinking how attracted I was to him, and wondering if he felt the same, if anything. He was such a gentleman. I was grateful he would help me this way. I had a quick shower in the attached bathroom, and then went to bed in one of his sister's teeny-bopper-styled long pajama tees that met me just above my knees. It felt a bit like being over at a friend's for a sleepover back years ago. Except I was alone. In Matt's condo mansion. And he was a few doors down. I remember I had no underwear on, and why, and then the memory of the fire came flooding back again. I had nothing. Not even underwear.

I drifted to sleep as my head hit the pillows thinking about him, and had wild, unsettling dreams about the fire, the press conference, and the Holstein's faces in that framed photo, as my subconscious weaved them through every scene.

~~ Chapter Eight ~~

I woke up to my own shrill screams from a horrible nightmare that seemed to take over my entire being. The sheets were twisted and crumpled in my hands and my body was drenched; I was shivering from a cold sweat, and my hair was matted down to the sides of my face. Just then, Matt rushed into the bedroom with a worried look on his face.

"What happened? Is everything alright?" he asked as he walked over to the side of the bed.

"Sorry for waking you," I replied, and sat up. "It was just a bad dream."

"Hold on," Matt said. He quickly left the room and came back a few moments later with a robe and a glass of water. He placed the water on the nightstand and sat on the edge of the bed. He wrapped the robe around me, keeping his arms resting on my shoulders as if to give me some emotional support. The robe was warm, and his touch was comforting. He had on a loose white t-shirt and cotton pajama pants. I leaned forward and he pulled me into his chest and held me, warming me with his embrace as my head came to rest on his shoulder.

"It's ok. Kate," he said reassuringly.

"It felt so, so real," I answered. "In the dream, I kept seeing their faces in the same bedroom I helped their son from. They were screaming to me, to save them too. And I reached out my hands for them to hold on, but they were too far away."

"It's ok," he said softly, stroking my back and drawing me closer to warm me up. He turned his face to me and kissed my hair softly. "You're safe. You're safe now. The nightmares are normal after the kind of trauma you went through. It'll get better. They'll pass, I promise."

His body heat radiated to my chilled, sweat-soaked body. It felt so warm, so inviting. As he kissed my cheek I couldn't resist that magnetism drawing me to him since we first met. And he smelled so good. I lifted my head, turned toward him and kissed his neck. My heart began to race. I was hot with a raw desire for him. He slid his hands up, cupped my face and kissed my lips softly. Every nerve in my body seemed to respond in synchronicity. He moved one hand to my waist, pulling me even closer as his tongue pushed the seam of my lips and parted my mouth. I responded and matched his tongue, my longing for him growing and making my clit throb.

I let out a low moan into his kiss, the desire overtaking any coherent thought that might have been taking place in my head. That moan may have driven him over the edge as well because he took hold of my waist and lifted me onto his lap in one strong motion. His ripped body was burning hot through his clothes and I could feel his rock-hard erection on my ass cheek. Without coming out of his kiss, I contorted my right leg and straddled him. He grabbed my hips and pulled me closer, his own hips rocking gently and leaving me feeling a desperate need for more. I was out of control. All I wanted was to feel him between my legs, ravishing me and filling me with his manhood.

In one fluid movement, he leaned forward and laid me on the bed with one arm while the other hand reached down to my leg and lifted my pajama top out of the way. I grabbed at his waist and wildly pulled his pants down, to feel his erection on me. He pulled my hands away and lifted them above my head. He pulled his mouth out of the kiss, panting heavily.

"God, you're so beautiful. Let me please you, Kate. Let me help you forget."

He tugged at my top and pulled it up past my breasts. When his tongue touched one of my hardened nipples, every part of my body pulsated. I let out a loud moan as he licked and sucked one nipple while stroking the other.

"I want you inside me, Matt," I said in a rhythmic purr. "I need you now."

His tongue travelled down my abdomen, heightening my desire for him to fuck me hard. He held himself up with one arm and reached his other hand down to my trembling, soaking wet pussy. He circled my clit with his thumb while his two fingers teased and tantalized me as they slid inside with prowess. My hips complied, rocking back and forth on his talented hand. I surrendered to his touch and yearned for him to enter me and drive me to unbridled ecstasy. The waves of pleasure took control of every inch of me, and my body shuddered in anticipation of the coming climax.

As my mind temporarily re-entered my body, it hit me that no one had ever made me this excited, this ravenous. It was a primitive, carnal, untamed need that had to be met, no matter what. I was still longing to feel him inside me when his lips reached my swollen clit. He licked my mound with intensified speed, his tongue tracing my grooves and flicking the tip as his fingers still danced wildly inside my channel.

"Yes, Matt, yes!" I squealed passionately. I fisted his hair and pulled his head deeper between my legs, wanting to feel his tongue and ride his fingers harder. I was at the pinnacle of pleasure. My head tilted back and my loud groan gave my intense climax away. It was like nothing I had ever felt before.

Matt slid his body up beside me and wrapped his arms around me protectively. My mind was still outside myself, as I snuggled into his warmth and rested my head on his welcoming chest. It took me some time to return to my senses. I panted to catch my breath and noticed him breathing deeply as his chest raised and lowered rhythmically.

"That was amazing," I said shyly.

"I'm glad I could make you feel better," he replied in a sleepy tone. "Water?" He reached over to the nightstand and passing the glass of water to me before I responded. I took the glass and tilted my head up to drink. I gulped at the water, realizing I was parched, and probably dehydrated.

"Thanks," I said once the glass was empty, placing it in his waiting hand for him to return it to the nightstand. He had a nurturing way about him. It seemed to be embedded into everything he did. It made me want him more. "Don't you want to keep going?"

"Trust me, there's nothing I want more right now, Kate," he answered in a low but kind tone. "I'm hard as hell and you felt so fucking good. So wet... I just have to get up in a couple of hours and I need to be alert. Big board meeting. And a big day for you."

"Alright," I said. "But now I feel like I really owe you."

"You don't owe me anything," he said softly, then smiled. "But you can let me take you out for a nice dinner after the ceremony tonight."

"Deal," I replied.

"I should let you rest now." He started slipping his arm from under me and I resisted.

"Stay with me," I asked. "Please, Matt?" I didn't care if I was begging. It just felt so good being close to him.

"Ok, but let me set the alarm clock," he said, sitting up to pick up the sleek, minimalist styled analog clock beside the empty glass. "I can't miss this meeting and it's at 8:00 a.m. sharp."

I snuggled up against him when he returned to his spot on the bed. I knew my carnal desires had overtaken my judgment, and any hesitation I might have had about being with the hero-type was shelved neatly in the recesses of my mind. He was right about helping me forget. I slept.

+++

When I woke up I was alone in the bed. I was disoriented for a few moments as the surroundings were so unfamiliar. Then it came back that I was at Matt's place, and what had happened the night before brought a silly smile on my face. God, he was good. I had to admit, he seemed genuine and may actually be a nice guy.

I got a brief look at the clock as I looked around the sun-filled room, and had to do a double-take. It was two o'clock in the afternoon! What time did I need to be at that ceremony? And how come no one called? Then I remembered. No cell phone. Shit.

I got out of bed and put the robe on, remembering how he held it around me when I woke up from the nightmare. I buried my nose into it and got a faint whiff of his cologne. I smiled and headed out the bedroom to see if he might be around. As I walked out into the hallway, I saw an older lady approaching. She had dark hair pulled back in a bun and was dressed in a maid's uniform. She walked toward me and held out three full-length clothing bags in one hand and four shopping bags in the other.

"Hello, Miss Samuel," she said in a South American Spanish accent. "I'm Yolanda. I work for Mr. Lewis. He wanted me to give this to you."

"Thanks, Miss Yolanda," I replied. "Pleased to meet you. And call me Kate."

"You too Miss Sam-uh Kate," she answered with a grin. "There are more things that came for you too. It's in the next room."

"Things like what?" I asked with curiosity.

"Clothes and shoes, and other things Mr. Lewis sent for you," she answered, as though it was completely normal for things to come to their place for me all the time. "Mister Lewis also asked me to wake you up at 2:30pm so you can be ready when Ross comes to pick you up."

"Ross?" I questioned.

"He's Mr. Lewis' driver," she replied. "He'll be downstairs waiting to take you to get your award."

"Oh. Ok. Thanks," I said. "I'd better get dressed. Oh, can I use the phone?"

"Yes, of course," she replied. "There's a cordless phone in your room. It's in the corner, on the vanity dresser."

"Thanks so much Yolanda," I said gratefully.

"No problem at all," she answered. "I'm so proud to meet you, Miss Samuel. You saved that boy, God bless your heart."

I nodded at her, then smiled as she walked away cheerfully to do her housework somewhere in that expansive place.

I decided to phone George on his cell to let him know where I was, and to check in as we hadn't spoken since during the Mayor's press conference. He didn't answer so I called Richard.

"Hello?" he answered.

"Richard, it's me Kate."

"Hi Kate. How are you feeling, honey?"

"Better today. I stayed at Matt's last night."

"Yes he left George a message. So is he hot? What's his place like?" Richard would have grilled me to no end so I got to the point quickly.

"I'll give you all the details later, Richard. Can you ask George to bring my purse when he comes to the ceremony? Everything was still at the station after I fainted."

"Yes of course. Not to worry it's at home. George brought it last night. Sorry, we weren't home early last night. We didn't realize you'd be released so quickly. We had gone out with some friends, and when we got back we saw Matt's messages. Sorry love."

"It's ok, really," I said, thinking I should be thanking them. It was their inadvertent absence that was instrumental in getting me that pleasure-filled, leave-me-wanting-more, passionate encounter with Matt. "I've gotta get ready for tonight. Will fill you in soon ok? See you, Richard."

"Bye love," he replied. "See you soon. I'll be cornering you to get the blow-by-blow, so don't you dare leave anything out, darling."

As he hung up, I smiled again, walking over to the bags Matt sent over. I figured I'd check the rest of the things the next day as there wasn't much time. The four shopping bags had two pairs of shoes, accessories of all types, and toiletries. And underwear! I was so relieved to see the dozen or so lacy numbers, wrapped in fine, scented paper from Victoria's Secret. I felt better. Having underwear was progress. It was a step closer to normalcy. It's amazing how those simple, little things come to have such significance when you're staring loss in the face. Still, I hadn't lost nearly as much as those Holstein kids. I wondered where they were, whether they were at least with family, and made a mental note to check the news later on to find out.

The contents of the three clothing bags completely threw me off guard. The first was a sleek, black strapless cocktail dress with an elegant silk trim at the waistband. It seemed too dressy for a Firefighter's award ceremony, but then again I hadn't ever been to one so how could I possibly know what was appropriate. In the second was a cream blazer with a slim black patent leather belt attached on the sides of its tapered waist. A matching black camisole and skirt were on a hanger in the same bag. This looked more like what a civilian might wear to such an event. The third was a floor-length, red strapless ball gown. There was an ornate, sequined pattern on the bodice, and it was flowing from the waist down. Definitely too dressy. The choice was made.

I took a shower and quickly got ready. The outfit fit me perfectly. I had to hand it to Matt for figuring out my size so accurately. There was also a nice selection of makeup in one of the shopping bags, so I wore a little lipstick and mascara. That was all I felt I could tolerate putting on as applying makeup wasn't something I regularly spent hours on. I took a quick look in the full-length closet mirror. Definitely put together, and hopefully not too vixen-like. I felt more rested. It was time to go.

Yolanda called up to me just as I was walking down the stairs to leave. She introduced me to Ross, who was waiting at the elevator for me, and we left.

~~ Chapter Nine ~~

The ceremony started promptly at 3:30p.m., about five minutes after I arrived. I was seated in the front row with other civilians and firefighters, presumably others being recognized to receive special awards. The Mayor and Fire Chief delivered their speeches and then the NYC Fire Marshal introduced the award recipients.

> "It is completely fitting, and gives me great pleasure to formally congratulate these firefighters and civilians who put their lives in danger to help so many others. Today's ceremony gives the people of New York City a chance to reflect on the role that firefighters and everyday heroes play in the community. We each owe these individuals a debt of gratitude for their selflessness, bravery, and care. These awards are a symbol of thanks for their special contribution.
>
> "For people like Miss Katherine Samuel, the recognition is all the more salient. At the time of the fire, this young lady witnessed the plight of young Joel Holstein and immediately assessed the scene and coordinated his rescue on her own, putting herself in danger and sustaining injuries herself. The self-driven decision for such people to take risks in such dangerous situation is never recommended, but they must always be applauded. It true humanity in action to risk your life to help someone in need."

He went on to recognize each person in the front row and then we were called up one by one to receive a plaque. That's when I noticed Matt was one of the firefighter recipients, but sat with his colleagues on the left side of the front row seats. After the ceremony I was swarmed by reporters, members of the public and other officials, all wanting to congratulate me, hug me or get a sound bite. I was so relieved when George and Richard approached the group, with Matt towering behind them. They flanked me on three sides and walked me out quickly.

"Thanks for the save," I said. "That was not something I was fully prepared to handle. Especially after seeing Joel Holstein and his sister were a couple rows behind me. I lost all my words. It's so sad."

"So true," Matt started, and wrapped both my hands with his to get my complete attention. "As firefighters, we struggle with that anytime there's a fatality. But you need to remind yourself that you gave him something he wouldn't have had - more time here on earth. Because of you he has time to grow up, to make mistakes, to fall in love, to have his own family, and maybe to help others. That's the legacy you created, so don't you ever feel to blame for what happened to his parents. They're somewhere out there thanking you for saving him."

Tears came to my eyes. What a kind soul, to try to help me that way. I really was a wreck those few days. Emotional, and weak, and vulnerable. And falling for Matt...

They led me out of the hall and agreed the four of us would go to dinner together. Ross was waiting outside and he let us all into the car, which was more of a stretch limousine. Before that day, I had not driven in one since I was back in Phoenix, and I hadn't missed the luxury... much.

Somehow at dinner, Richard managed to lighten the mood for all of us. He told comedic stories of his awkward childhood, playing out entire scenes like he was the leading man in a Broadway show. He joked about George's quirks, which were numerous, and I knew, as I worked with him. He even got up and sang his rendition of 'I will Survive' when the song came up on the old-styled Muzac system at the restaurant. I laughed so hard at one point that I sounded like I was in a coughing or crying fit. Looking back, it was just the medicine I needed.

It was George who brought the communal mood to a more somber tone when he raised the fire disaster. "It's really sad about the Holsteins, isn't it?" he asked. "I can just imagine what the kids are going through."

"Who were those people at the funeral?" I asked. "The ones taking care of the kids."

"Family I think," said Richard. "Do you realize that almost a hundred people were affected by the fire?"

"Probably more," Matt chimed in. "There was some damage to the roofs of the apartment complex on the end of the street. We had to relocate ten families from those building units while we surveyed the damage."

"What a shame," George responded. "Such a bad time for this to happen."

We all nodded. "So what caused the fire in the first place?" I asked.

"We're still investigating, but it'll likely be classified as arson," Matt replied. "I can't get into it, but there were some unusual things we found in unit 16."

"What?" Richard exclaimed. "So you mean the Holstein's death wasn't accidental?"

"That's not what I said," Matt replied defensively, probably realizing he had told us too much. "I really can't say any more. We're still looking into it. I think the most important thing to focus on now is helping the families."

"Well that's something we can definitely work on at the station," answered George.

"They need everything," said Matt." Better shelter than the hotels most of them are staying at, food supplies, clothing and other essentials."

"Man, that's tough," Richard said.

"Many of them had to leave their homes basically with the clothes they were wearing at the time," Matt said.

"Well I know we can help," George replied. "The station is holding a food and donation drive starting tomorrow, and we're already getting calls. We partnered with the local Red Cross and Salvation Army, and listeners can drop the food donations off at the Sally-Ann just down the street."

"That's great of you, man," Matt answered in encouragement. "I've started to get some things moving through one of my family's foundation, but it takes a village, right?"

"So true, Matt. And a listener also let us know about a trust fund set up for the kids," George continued. "It's at the Bank of New York Mellon down the street."

"Send me the details by email and we'll see what we can do," Matt replied. "Actually, I'm hosting a charity ball in a week. I think we can add this campaign to the fundraising effort that night. If the three of you are free, I would love for you to attend."

"Oooh a charity ball," Richard exclaimed with delight. "George and I would be honored to come, Matt. Kate, you'll be all better by then. You've gotta come too, darling."

"Sure. I'd love to come, especially if it'll help more people," I answered. "Can you send me the details by email? I'd like to help them too. Poor kids..." I trailed off again, thinking about them.

George took that opportunity to break up the discussion, explaining he and Richard had to go back to the station, as there was an issue with the staffing roster. "We've been fielding a ton of calls from people who want to help the families who were displaced by the fire," he explained. "The real issue is what kind of temporary housing they'll be able to find at this time of year. It's like you said, Matt. After a while, a family of 4 in a cramped up hotel just becomes a little too much."

"I can come and help," I offered.

George had insisted that I take another few days off to feel better, and suggested that staying at Matt's would probably allow me to get more rest. I didn't put up much resistance, especially since my new sets of underwear were there. That fact – having my own underwear - more or less made Matt's place feel like a bit of home. Still, I didn't want to impose so I suggested I could stay at a hotel.

"Are you crazy?" said Matt. "That's not an option. You need to be somewhere safe and you need someone around. Yolanda is at the condo every day and she's very sweet. Plus I've got lots of room."

"I have my purse now," I countered. "I can stay somewhere close to the radio station. Besides, I have to start looking for my own place while I figure out what will happen with the insurance, or rebuilding, or whatever the plans will be."

"No," he replied firmly as though I was a kid and his say was final. "You need to stay with me. Just stay for the holidays. And when you get better in a few days, you can go house-hunting to be in your new place for the New Year."

His insistence was beginning to sound like demands and it was something I really disliked, but I also knew deep down that he was right. The last thing I wanted was to pass out in a hotel room with no one around to get me to help.

He saw my reaction and gave me a broad, irresistible smile. "C'mon. Don't make me have to use the fireman's carry on you."

"Alright, alright," I replied. "But just one week and not a day longer."

"Not acceptable," he persisted. "This is the worse time of year to be alone. You're staying and the discussion is over."

"Matt, I'm not your staff, you know?" I half-shouted. "Why do you think any of this makes sense? I mean, I barely know you."

"You weren't saying that last night," he joked. That broad, confident smile was a powerful aphrodisiac, and he was growing on me, but I knew I had to stand my ground. Something about his offer to help, briefly reminded me of my own parents, using *things* and *comforts* to lure me into compliance. It might have been in my own head, but I was not going to be controlled, even at this low point.

"Look, Matt.," I said firmly. "I appreciate the gesture. You've been so kind and I can't thank you enough. But I'm making it a week at most, or I'll just go to the hotel now."

"Ok. You win. One week," he conceded. "But I reserve the right to tempt you repeatedly to get you to stay.

"And why is that? I questioned. "Why are you so insistent that I stay?"

"You really want to know?"

"Yes. What is it?"

"The truth is..." He hesitated. "No one should be alone when they're down and out. No one. Including you. Especially you. You almost gave *your life* to save that boy! You just got out of the hospital yesterday. And the media won't stop hounding you for a while. How can anyone let you be alone now?"

That's it? Hero Hospitality? Bah.

"Well, that and you're cute when you black out," he joked as though reading my mind. He grabbed my waist, pulling me closer with both hands as we stood in the doorway of the restaurant. He leaned over and gently kissed my forehead. "C'mon it's so cold out. Let's go home."

Home.

He took my hand and led me over to the car. Ross was already waiting with a door open. The ride home was quiet, but charged with sexual tension. I could feel the energy vibrating off his body and searing right through to my crotch. It was so strong I felt like I was buzzing. We didn't speak or touch or make eye contact.

+++

As we walked off the elevator into his condo, he stopped short. "Wait. Sit here in the living room. I have something for you."

"You got me a room full of things that I haven't even looked at, Matt. You don't need to get me anything else."

"Shhh. Just sit and wait." He ducked into the large dining room beside the expansive kitchen. I could hear him digging through something metal. He returned with his hand behind his back and a warm smile on his chiseled face.

"Close your eyes," he instructed me.

"What is it?" I resisted. "Just show me."

"Just close 'em," he persisted.

As I closed my eyes, I felt his hands, as well as something cold, brush against the sides and back of my neck. He then fumbled with what I figured was a clasp, then gently place his hands on my shoulder. My body tingled from his touch.

"Ok," he continued. "You can open your eyes now."

When I opened my eyes he was kneeling in front of me as I sat on the sofa. I touched my neck and traced my fingertips on the piece of jewelry. Once I touched the pendant, I knew what it was. I jumped out of the chair and rushed toward the floor-to-ceiling mirrors at the entrance to see if it was really what I thought. It was the necklace that my grandmother gave to me when I was twelve, just before she died. With everything that happened during the last couple of days, I hadn't thought about all the things had been wiped out during the fire. How could I not have remembered this piece? It was clearly singed but intact. I felt a burst of joy rising up from the depths of my stomach.

"Oh my God, how did you find this!" I choked and squeaked, and my voice trembled, not able to hold in how emotion-filled I was as I walked back over to him in the living room.

"I was on-site with the Fire Marshall's investigative team today," he explained. I thought I'd see what I could recover from your place. The box it was in was all warped and melted, but the necklace was fine. Just a little smoke and soot on it. Yolanda can shine that right up."

"This belonged to my great, great grandmother," I started. "And probably went a few more generations back, too. There's been a tradition for it to be handed down every second generation, so my grandmother gave it to me. My grandma once said it might be worth tens of thousands of dollars, but it's not about that value at all. It meant so much to me to have a piece of her with me. I can't believe you found it. I, I just don't know how to thank you, Matt."

As he stood up, I reached up and around his broad shoulders. We shared the warmest embrace. I was probably a little overzealous, peppering him with kisses all over his face and neck. He was smiling broadly again, and accepting every kiss with glee.

"It's the least we could do. The building isn't structurally sound anymore, so we weren't able to keep looking. Sorry I couldn't find more for you and..."

"No, no, this is everything I could ever want, Matt," I cut him off, teary-eyed with joy. "Everything else was replaceable. They're just meaningless stuff. But this, I don't know how I'll ever repay you for finding this. Thank you Matt."

I laced my hands around his neck and through his hair, feeling so attracted to him. He was irresistible and I was in the moment. I tiptoed and closed my eyes as I tilted my head forward to kiss his tempting lips. He met my mouth with just as much desire, and soon his hands were around my waist, pulling me closer. The kiss was raw and full of need, making my pussy throb with passion. As he towered over me in height, I felt his rock-hard shaft press through his pants onto my waist. I was wet and ready to drop all my inhibitions.

"I don't want you to think you have to do this, Kate," he mumbled in a husky voice, in between breaths as we maintained the arousing kiss.

"I know," I said softly, allowing my pussy to take complete control of my brain. I nuzzled his ear with my lips and whispered, "I want to. I want you, Matt. Make love to me."

~~ Chapter Ten ~~

Our eyes never lost contact with each other as he lowered me on the living room sofa. I shuddered with anticipation for a moment. What was it about him that was so compelling? Everything. Not only was he strikingly good-looking, he was also kind. Thoughtful. Empathetic. And yes, he was a firefighter, but he was so much more. He had a heart and seemed genuine. And for the life of me I hadn't sensed any ego, or at least, none that I had seen so far. And yes, he was clearly wealthy, but that was not something that had made him any more appealing in my eyes. I left that life once, and it was not something I was looking for. Everything else about him was just... right.

His lips descended onto mine and there was no more coherent thought. I yearned to taste him and be teased as he parted my lips and crushed his tongue into mine. I felt his solid cock press against me and grabbed his firm ass to feel him closer. He quickly propped himself up on one arm and used the other to start unbuttoning my blazer. I helped him frantically, reaching the back of my bra to unsnap it as my blazer fell to the floor, not wanting to slow the pace of our heated rhythm. I needed to feel his heat and be skin-to-skin with him. He quickly pulled out of the kiss, then grabbed my arm gently and stood up.

"I want to see you, Kate" he whispered. "I just want to look at you for a minute. Let me take all your clothes off."

I nodded and he removed the rest of my clothes, slowly dropping them to the floor one by one. When I was completely naked he just stood and watched me with a dreamy look in his eyes.

"You're so beautiful Kate," he said. "I could watch you all night."

He came closer and cupped my face, reaching in for a passionate kiss. His touch was gentle, and seemed filled with both longing and some reverence. It was like fondling your favorite toy, not wanting to damage it, but unable to resist the urge to touch it. I couldn't stand the waiting anymore. My pussy was throbbing so hard, I grabbed his shirt and unbuttoned them frenetically, then undid his belt and dragged his pants down with his briefs. His cock was massive. And it was so hard he looked like he would burst.

As I kissed him, we descended into our own sacred and primitive world. All that was present was need, attraction, heat and desire. I took his hand and pressed it onto my burning hot mound, desperately wanting to feel him inside me. He went wild. He kissed me deeply and slid two fingers into my channel. He explored my mouth with his tongue, moving it at the same pace that he flicked my clit with his thumb. There was no more control. Just untamed, animal instinct.

"I want you so bad, Kate," he finally said, letting out a deep moan as he released me from the kiss and moved his lip down to my breasts. My nipples were already hard, and his touch intensified my erotic insanity beyond what I could bear. I wrapped my legs around his back, drawing him in. I needed to feel his hot, hard shaft inside my channel and my body refused to wait.

"Come inside me, Matt," I said longingly. "I need you to fill me up and make me come."

"I need you too, baby," he moaned, reaching over to his pants pocket and pulling out a condom. The package was ripped open and the condom slipped onto his raging erection in record speed. His eyes were fixated and brimming over with pure, sexual hunger and rabid desire. It was contagious, as I wanted him so badly. My clit was so inflamed in the arousal I couldn't wait anymore. I gently pushed against his chest so he would sit up. He moved willingly, and I positioned myself on top of him, with my knees straddling each side and facing him.

I started lowering onto his shaft slowly, but he was just as needy. He grabbed my ass cheeks with both hands and pulled me down on his cock with such force it felt like hot lightning shooting into me. My eyes rolled back into my head as I rode him, bracing myself by holding onto his shoulders. And he took full advantage of the position, slowly sucking on each breast. It was raw and wild and untamed. And we both wanted more.

He licked and teased them one by one, then alternated between biting them gently then blowing. As I felt his hot breath on my nipples, unbridled need kept rising and brimming over inside me. Every lick, every touch was driving me further into the primitive pleasure of the erotic escape. He grabbed my ass tighter and closer into him, and his large hands felt so warm and inviting. He squeezed my ass cheeks and reached closer to my opening, grabbing so tightly and making me wetter with every thrust. His fingers spread my lips so I could take him even deeper into me. When he let out a low groan, that sound drove me completely insane and set my climax in full-steam-ahead motion.

"Oh, God Matt, I'm coming!" I moaned out loud. My channel tightened and clenched violently onto his shaft, sending him into his own climactic release as he kept rocking me on his own ride to ecstasy. Slowly, he relieved his grip and wrapped his arms around my waist tightly. He nuzzled his head into my neck and we held each other for quite some time, before any words would come.

"You were amazing," he said first, holding me tightly in his warm embrace.

"You too," I replied, still basking in the mindless glow.

"You're so warm, so responsive, so giving, Kate," he whispered in my ear. I could feel his cock begin to harden inside me and I was starting to tingle with the needy sensation again. He leaned forward and stood up, holding me firmly to keep my legs wrapped around him. I held on with my arms locked around his neck, licking and teasing his ear lobe. He gently lifted me off of his hardness and started walking toward the stairs with me in his arms. He was so strong, holding me as if I was as light as a baby. His baby.

Hero salvation.

"I'd better get us upstairs and get you to bed, Kate," he said as he began to return to his senses. "Before my raging hormones take over again. I'll grab these things in the morning."

I nodded and he shifted me around so my legs were on his right forearm.

"I can still walk, you know?" I said, noticing he wasn't putting me down.

"Yes I guess you can," he replied with his ravishing smile. "But I'm not taking any chances. You're getting put to bed, young lady. No fainting for you."

"Yes sir, Lieutenant Lewis, sir!" I replied, and motioned my hand in salute.

"And don't you make fun of the guy carrying your sexy ass," he joked.

I winked as he walked up the steps effortlessly, in awe of his protective and giving nature. All my defenses were down and I realized that my heart was already at the point of no return. But it didn't matter anymore. If my heart was going to be dragged through the mud later, it was totally worth it. It had only been a few days since Matt came into my life and he had been there from the fire and at every point since then.

He was with me in the hospital. Saved me from the reporters at Richard and George's place, and then took care of me until they came home. He had caught my fall after I fainted at the press conference, stayed with me at the hospital. He had fed me, gave me a place to stay and put clothes on my back. He rescued me from the barrage of media at the ceremony.

And he'd found my grandmother's necklace. All for me. What else did I need to know that he was genuinely a nurturer and a protector? Nothing. I knew enough. I was going to trust my gut and just let him treat me with the kindness my nana said I deserved from the man that would one day be mine. As lofty and pie-in-the-sky as that sounded – and it did sound like a load of old-styled, fantasy bullshit, because who even talked like that anymore? – I believed it.

Fallen for the Hero.

As he got to the top of the stairs, he was heading into my room and I stopped him. "I want to stay with you, Matt. I don't want to be alone tonight. I need to feel you close to me." I didn't care how desperate or vulnerable I sounded. It was the truth. I needed his tenderness and his strength enveloping me.

He moaned deeply and kissed my ear. He continued past the room with the things he bought me, and over to what was clearly the master bedroom. The room was dark, but the hallway lights were on. I could see the décor seemed bright and contemporary, with a modern, minimalist influence. None of that mattered. It could have been a kid's room with a Hot Wheels bed, for all I cared. I was going to be with him. Safe. Protected. Loved.

He placed me down gently on one side of the king sized bed and walked over to his closet. "Here's a robe for you. You'll need this in the morning. Yolanda comes in pretty early and she's used to barging into my room like I'm still five years old. She's been our housekeeper for a very long time."

"Ok," I replied softly. "Thanks, Matt."

"I'll be right back," he said. "I'll go get our clothes now, just in case she comes in before I wake up. I don't want her to feel uncomfortable."

As he left I looked at his delicious ass and huge, majestic frame. God, was he ever a specimen. I imagined all the ways he could rock my world, from A to Z, a hundred ways till Sunday, and then start all over again. My body arousal switch was turned on and nothing was shutting it down. I lay back in his bed and rolled over onto my stomach. My eyes closed as I buried my head in his pillow to smell his scent, just as he walked back in.

"So," he started, walking over to the armchair near the window and placing our clothes on it. "I'm off shift tomorrow, and not a thing in my calendar. You know what that means?"

"What?" I asked.

"I'm yours all day," he said, with his eyes wide and eyebrows raised. That sounded so good.

"Well, then," I replied playfully. "I'll just have to think up some things I can do to you."

"Seriously though, you should rest," he cautioned. "You need rest to get better."

"Ahh, so then keep me in bed all day, Lieutenant," I teased with the same tone he had used just moments earlier.

"I can't refuse that offer," he said as he caved. "But you're getting some rest too."

"Deal," I said with a smile. A long yawn came out of me from nowhere. I guess I really was tired.

He came over to my side and pulled the covers up and over me. He bent down and kissed my forehead gently, then walked over to his side and lay down. I snuggled up to him and he seemed only too happy to wrap his huge arms around me. My eyes closed and within what seemed like seconds, I was asleep.

~~ Chapter Eleven ~~

When I woke up, the light was pouring in through Matt's east-facing windows. For a few fleeting moments, I buried my face under the pillow, trying to hold on to the escape of dreamless and restful sleep. His sheets were high thread count Egyptian cotton and so comfy, with a slight smell of fresh rain and Matt. In his massive master bedroom, it felt like heaven. Even the pillows smelled like brand new cotton and fabric detergent.

I turned over and noticed that Matt wasn't in bed anymore. In the distance, I heard the muffled sound of the shower behind closed doors so I figured it was him. With a short groan, I turned with the pillow and slowly sat up. His nightstand had a similar clock as my room, and it was just after 8:30 a.m. A few minutes later, with my eyes still a little glazed with sleep, Matt came out of the shower. His well-chiseled face was split with the broadest grin.

"Morning, sunshine!" His large, rugged hands ran through his wet hair, which rebounded back in resistance to its original position. He seemed his usual positive and jovial self.

"I think it's going to be a beautiful day," he proclaimed, in a voice as chipper as the birds that would sing outside my window when I was on the farm in Phoenix. As he walked over to his windows and looked out, I swung my legs over the side of the bed. I stretched and let out a long yawn.

"I couldn't agree more," I replied. My voice was still raspy with sleep.

"So you were the Arizona bourgeoisie, weren't you?" he asked from the window, without looking back at me.

"What do you mean?" I asked, not sure why he asked that out of the blue.

"Well, just listen to how you talk," he answered. "Your speech still has the rounded tones of having completed finishing school somewhere. Trust me, I would know. My sister and I have been there, done that and got the posh t-shirts."

"Well, yes," I replied, smiling and pushing my tousled hair out of my eyes. "It was unavoidable. Luckily, I got the honor of appending a nice New York accent to it."

Grinning, Matt walked over to me and planted a big kiss on my hair. The sunlight shone through his hair as I looked up at him, making him seem angelic and edible. "And it sounds like pretty Yankee heaven, my dear."

I tilted my head up and descended his mouth into mine for a long, tender kiss. I held him around his neck and slid my fingers through his wet hair, which brought me to full arousal so quickly. He smelled so good, and that made me remember I hadn't yet showered.

"I'll be right back," I said, pulling out of the kiss. "A nice, long shower is calling my name."

"Want some company?" he asked, with a slightly upturned smile.

"Sure," I answered. It was an irresistible offer as far as I was concerned. The advance sent a shiver of anticipation through my body.

He took my hand and led me into his bathroom. It took my breath away. The bathroom was large enough to do yoga poses in, and probably a couple of cartwheels. The spacious shower stall was large and flush with the floor, with tempered glass doors from floor to ceiling. And inside it was also a dramatic boulder rock for seating. It was pretty obvious that Matt had this room redone to his masculine style. The colors were earth tones, with natural lighting and textured tiles. And it was topped off with a steam shower. Sweet Jesus, was it ever decadent.

He might have read my mind because he rested his hands on my shoulder and said, "Yup. This is my fave space in the whole condo. I spend a lot of time in here, so it was the only place I redecorated when my parents passed."

"It's just, gorgeous," I replied, wondering why a guy would admit to spending a lot of time in the bathroom. Admire yourself much?

He turned on the shower and I stepped in. The deliciously warm water rejuvenated my tired body. Matt stepped in behind me and started to scrub my back with a bath sponge. Could this be what heaven was like? I turned toward him and stopped short for a moment, admiring his delightfully perfect body. For a moment, I couldn't believe I was in this fantastic place with such an incredibly hot fireman.

Hero worship.

I traced my hand down his chest, lingering slowly to feel his rock hard pecs and rippling abs. He guided my hand down to his completely erect shaft and slid his fingers to explore my already throbbing clit. I let out a long moan, and he lifted me up in one swift motion. My legs wrapped instinctively around his hips, impatient for his cock to slide inside me. In three long strides, he was at the wall of the shower. He propped me up against it and in a single thrust, his long, hard shaft was buried inside my hot, clenched channel.

"Fuck me hard, Matt," I groaned to him in a sultry voice I barely recognized. It was like I was temporarily possessed by a nymphomaniac who couldn't ever get enough sex.

"God, Kate, you're so tight and wet, baby," he answered as the water lapped our upper bodies and splashed everywhere from our jerking motion. "Fuck, I didn't wear a condom."

"It's ok baby," I said quickly, enjoying feeling his bare cock inside me rocking over and over again. I was well past any sense of care about the logistics of protective sex. "I'm on the pill, and I'm 100% clean."

"Fuck! I think I'm gonna come," he exclaimed. He thrust his shaft deeper inside me, filling my space and then some. As he said those words it triggered my orgasmic rush. My head tilted back in complete escape. I felt his rhythm speed up without warning. In one long, hard thrust I felt his body shudder and then his release deep inside me.

"I don't know what you do to me, Kate," he said after he recovered. Our eyes locked on each other, and I could see this tender, gentle gaze in his eyes. It gripped at my heart. Hard. All I wanted to do was take care of him and agree to whatever he would ever ask of me. Any man who could look at a woman in that vulnerable, honest way, had to be deserving of a woman's complete and all-encompassing love.

He lowered me so my feet touched the floor, yet kept me pinned against the shower wall. Warm, steamy water flowed down our bodies as we stood there. It was surreal. Once we gathered up our senses, we finished our shower in silence but smiled at each other whenever we made eye contact.

+++

"Hey, you should go check the stuff in the next room and find something comfortable to wear," Matt said as we dried ourselves off in his bedroom. "I want to take you for breakfast. Well, more like brunch. You need to eat. And I'm beyond starved."

"Okay," I replied. "You know, you didn't need to buy me all that stuff."

"That was nothing," he answered. "I just had Ross swing by our Holt's store downtown. The girls were more than happy to get those together for New York's newest hero."

"Holts?" I asked, sliding into the robe he had put out for me. But what I really wanted to ask about was the girls. What girls?

"Yeah. We're a major shareholder in Holts," he answered. "It's not the best brand, but it's up there."

"Nice," I replied, a little distracted. I was still thinking about the girls he mentioned. What the hell was wrong with me, feeling a pang of jealousy at the mere mention of another female?

"And the clothes are of excellent quality. We carry a lot of the other designer labels too. My mom really loved their stuff."

"Awww, that's sweet," I answered as if my responses were on auto-pilot.

"Go on," he encouraged, and then smiled his broad, playful smile. "Before my hard-on kicks in again."

I smiled and walked out into the hall toward the room.

"Check it out. I hope there's enough to choose from."

I let out a soft gasp when I walked into the spare room. It was almost filled to the rafters. Racks upon racks of designer dresses, tops, pants, furs and winter coats stood in rows as though I was in a department store. All manner of shoes and winter boots were laid out on top of their resect5ve boxes, just waiting for their new owner to try on for size. It was sweet of Matt to get these for me, but it was way too much stuff.

I looked through the pants rack and pulled out a pair of straight-leg blue jeans. I found a simple, white cashmere sweater in the tops section – it really was too much – and walked back into my room to get dressed. As I got out in the hall, I heard loud noises coming from downstairs. I was concerned because it sounded like a heated argument. I didn't recognize the female voice, but then again, I only knew Ross and Yolanda from Matt's world.

Looking back, it probably wasn't a good idea to have gone downstairs in just my robe. Matt and a woman about my age were in an animated argument. So animated I couldn't understand a word they said as they talked and screamed over each other. I couldn't see her face as her back was turned. What I did see was that she was dressed to the nines in designer labels from head to toe.

As I approached them they stopped mid-sentence. She turned around. It was Joy.

"What the fuck is she doing here, Matt?" Joy asked, and glared at me.

"I should be asking *you* that, Joy," I replied quickly. Probably too quickly. "Why are you here?"

"Not that it's any of your fucking business, tramp," she started. "I'm Matt's girlfriend."

+++
TO BE CONTINUED
(Get the first 2 chapters of Book 2 below)

Liked HERO? Please leave an honest and fair review where you downloaded it, so more new adult and contemporary romance readers can find it!

Next in the series:

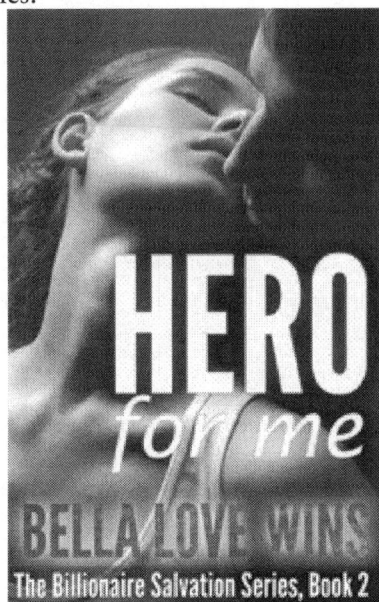

Join my Exclusive Reader list! You are just one click away.

Follow the link below and enter your email address to and get notified for freebies and more Hero titles once they are off the press.

>>>**Click here to get FRESH Hero freebies and updates**<<<

Once again, thank you, I hope you enjoy it!

Sincerely,

Bella Love-Wins

Website: http://bellalovewins.com/

Twitter: @BellaLoveWins

Facebook: https://www.facebook.com/BellaLoveWins

Wattpad: http://www.wattpad.com/user/BellaLoveWins

HERO For Me

(A Complimentary Sample of the First Two Chapters)
+++
The Billionaire Salvation Series, Book 2
Bella Love-Wins

~ She was hoping for a hero, but never realized who she would save. ~

~~ Chapter One ~~

Two days had already passed since I had last seen Matt, and the pain was still lurking. After Joy had showed up at his place, I didn't wait to hear another word from either of them. I had quickly run back to the guest room, put on what comfortable clothes I could find, grabbed my purse, and left.

When I had gotten back down to the elevator, Joy was gone. Matt kept repeating that he could explain, and it felt like I was reliving Chad Bridges all over again. So much so, that I refused to hear him out. I stood at the elevator, waiting for it to return so that I could escape. Matt insisted that it was a simple misunderstanding, and if I would only stop and listen to hear him out, that I would not need to leave. I couldn't.

I had to get away. There really was nothing that he could have said that would convince me to give him a chance. What more did I need to know? Matt and Joy were an item. The last thing that I wanted to be was the other woman. Sure, it felt good being with him, but that was before I had this new information.

Finally, the elevator had arrived, so I could get as far away from him as possible. I had asked the concierge to call a cab to take me home. I still had nowhere to go, but I knew that I could take care of that quickly enough. There were two decent hotels around the corner from the radio station, so I directed the taxi driver to the one that was closest. With just a purse and its contents as my only remaining possessions, I checked in and went to the room that the hotel receptionist assigned.

The room was quaint; however I knew that it was the best choice, if I had to be there for longer than a month. I had no idea what would happen with the insurance for the old place and in what timing, so I knew I had to rely on my savings to get by in the meantime. One good thing about the hotel was its proximity to the radio station. As I had begun to think about it, I realized I really missed my job. It had only been a few days that I was away, and with everything that had happened, from the fire, to the hospital, to Matt, I hadn't had much time to notice.

The very day that I left Matt's place, I had gone into work. George was surprised and felt I really should have been resting. Still, he was happy to see me because of how busy things had become. The station was gearing up for the holiday food drive and fundraiser, and they were shorthanded. I spent the rest of that first day organizing the food donations, and researching content and communities on social media to help get the word out.

Thankfully, because it was so busy, George didn't ask me a thing about Matt. He welcomed me to stay with him and Richard again, but this time, I really needed to be on my own, and he understood.

The shift flew by as usual. It was a refreshing distraction from the chaos of the prior few days. It was also such a relief to get outside for the short walk back to the hotel. As I walked through the hotel lobby, one of the reception desk staff waved at me to come to speak to her.

"Is there something you need?" I asked her.

"No, ma'am" she answered. "I just wanted to let you know that you received a substantial delivery. As we don't have a lot of storage, we placed it all in the room that joins with yours, and opened the adjoining door so you could access it."

"What kind of delivery?" I inquired further. I had not ordered anything to be delivered, so I was confused.

"It's from Matt Lewis, ma'am," she answered. "And he also prepaid for your room, well now it's two rooms, and it's paid for until the end of January."

"Who authorized you to do such a thing?" I asked, with a slight irritation in my tone, surprised that the hotel would allow this.

"Well ma'am," she explained, "Mr. Lewis' company owns this hotel."

"Oh," I answered, annoyed. "Well I certainly hope you won't be handing over my room key to Mr. Lewis should he ask you for it. Will you? Please let me know now, so I can check out if needs be, and go to a place where I will have complete privacy."

"Certainly not ma'am," she answered. "I mean, yes he does, as the owner of the hotel, have the ability to access your room, however I don't believe he will disregard your request. I'll make a note not to have anyone disturb you or deliver anything to you for the rest of your stay."

"I appreciate that," I stated firmly. "Thank you."

My blood was boiling. I know that hotels would deliver items to people's rooms. This was just too much. It all reminded me of my parents' control. Matt may have meant well, but the invasion only served to make me resent him and his power. I was tempted to look up another hotel and move immediately. My gut told me it was probably a wasted effort, because he would probably own half of the other places in this area, or would know the people who did.

Having come from that life, I knew with certainty how small the circle of power really is. What most people didn't know is that less than 50 families around the world control over 80% of all of the Western world's assets. I decided to stay put, but I refused to enter that adjoining room or to use a single item from it. Instead, I went back out to one of the neighboring boutiques, and bought my own clothes, shoes and other things I needed. I was not going to have him think I could be bought.

I kept busy the next day. There really was nothing that I should've expected from Matt, and honestly, there was no one to blame but myself. I had just presumed Matt was available and good God, look at him. A man so insanely attractive had to have been taken. I wouldn't say that I was heart-broken. It was more of a disappointment. I was numb. Maybe a little confused. The events of the last few days alone, without Matt in the picture, could explain how I was feeling. I knew, though, that Matt was a factor, so there was no use denying it.

Every time I thought about Matt, nausea would rise up to my throat. It's not that I felt he betrayed me. There was nothing to betray. I'd only known him for two days. Still, there were points where I felt I couldn't function. Like something was broken. He had been growing on me, but I had no explanation for how I was feeling. We were just getting to know each other, and there I was, like a bundle of frayed nerve endings.

Maybe a part of it was the loss of hope. I had to admit, I was beginning to hope for something to blossom between Matt and me, before I learned about Joy. Hope is one of those intangible feelings. It's something that could make you live an entire lifetime in one moment. It's like those science fiction movies, where we have carbon copies of ourselves in many different dimensions.

Hope can be a window, where you can see one possible you, and the path of your whole life and the people around you in the blink of an eye. My pain, then, must have been my mourning the loss of that one possible future, where there might have been something special between Matt and me. Whatever it was, I needed to get a fucking grip. I admitted I was being foolish, and just had to accept that he was not The One.

Over those last few days, with the fire and everything else, I had gotten used to not being online and not checking my texts and messages. As liberating as it was, I felt disconnected. I decided I would take that evening to clear out my inboxes and social media accounts, say hello to a few people, and reply where possible. I ordered room service, then sat on the sofa to start on the text messages first. Most were contacts from the media, and easy to delete. A few were from old college and high school friends, congratulating me and checking to see if I was ok. I noticed one of the more recent messages was from Matt, and said:

"Hi Kate. It's Matt. I'm really sorry. Please give me a chance to explain."

I hesitated for a moment, and then deleted it. I didn't want an explanation. I wanted a single man that I was attracted to, that felt the same way for me, so I could at least get to know him better. Was that a lot to ask? Probably.

I got through the rest of the text messages, deleting all except for two. The first was from a journalist from the New York Times. I had always dreamt of working for them when I was back in high school and college. I decided I would keep that message, more as a momento than anything else. The second was a strange note from a number I didn't recognize, and without a name. It simply said,

"Kate Rock. When will you be back for #newsrockcontest?"

I didn't know what to make of it. I had all my coworkers' numbers in my phone, so their names would have shown up beside the message, if it had been one of them. None of our listeners ever had access to our contact information. I decided I'd keep this message and ask George about it the next day.

Next to tackle were voice messages. I made myself comfortable on the sofa beside the bed, kicking off my shoes and resting my legs across the armrest. I got into a nice routine of listening and deleting the bulk of the messages, as they were mostly media requests. The last one was from Matt, and my heart tugged for a moment, from what he said.

"Kate, it's me, Matt. Listen, I'd really like to explain about Joy. In person. Face-to-face. It's not what you think. Give me a call when you can."

Deleting his message was a little harder to do. What could there be to explain? What did he mean that it wasn't what I thought? It's either he was in a relationship with Joy or not. He never said he was not in a relationship as I had stood waiting at the elevator. He just kept repeating that he could explain. And to me, that meant they were together.

I took a deep breath and went onto Facebook. There were too many posts, tags and messages to process. I put up a short note in my news feed to thank everyone for their kind words and support. I also directed them to visit the radio station website or Facebook page so they could support the food drive or donate. I checked the messages people left, and deleted most of them, including one from Matt that was similar to the text that he had sent. Deleting that one was easier. I reminded myself that in a couple of days I'd been over it all. Time had a way with these emotions. Somehow, deep down, I wasn't fully convinced. I sighed aloud and re-focused on the task.

There was a knock on the door and a call from the person on the other side, announcing it was my room service order. I went over to the door and looked through the peephole. You couldn't be too careful in these New York hotels these days. It was a hotel server, dressed in black and white with a white apron. As I opened the door, he wheeled the meal into my room on a cart, and then turned to leave without handing me a bill to sign.

"Did you forget the bill, sir?" I asked politely. It had become second nature for me to address server staff that way. My parents had had a tendency to be mean to our maids, drivers and the butler – actually they were rude to anyone they thought were not in their social class – so I did the opposite. I had seen how kind my grandmother was to our house staff, and decided I wanted to be like her. She was nothing, if not kind and humane.

"There's no bill, ma'am," he answered. "I was given instructions that anything sent to this room was not to have any charge to the occupant. I mean to you, ma'am."

"Alright," I answered. I knew there was no point in arguing with him. Matt was making his presence felt, but in a way I resented. If he had known me better, he wouldn't do all these things. To many other females, his gestures would probably have been met with blushes, smiles and cheer. It was a shame he didn't know me. All of his effort was fodder for me to like him less, which made me feel even less emotionally bruised. I could have thanked him for making it easier to get over it.

~~ Chapter Two ~~

I probably dozed off after eating, because I was abruptly awoken to the sound of someone knocking on the door. I walked over and was sure to look through the peephole again this time, because the knocking was fairly loud. I should have known. It was Matt. For a brief moment, I thought I would just not answer at all. How would he know if I was not at home? Then I remembered he owned the place and would probably be able to check. I then heard him call out to me.

"Kate, are you all right?" he asked, his voice sounding muffled through the doorway.

Without opening the door I answered through it. "I'm fine, Matt. And I don't want to talk to you. Can you just go away?"

"Hello Kate," he persisted, "I'm really glad to hear you're okay. I've been knocking for a few minutes. Sorry if it got loud."

He paused, waiting for my response. I didn't say a word.

"Hopefully I didn't wake you up?" he continued. I had nothing to say.

"Look, I don't want to have to talk to you like this, with a wall between us. Can you please just open the door, and give me five minutes?"

"I wish you would respect what I asked and just leave, Matt," I answered heatedly. I did not want to talk to him, listen to him, or lay eyes on that gorgeous face or smoking hot body. I think I knew deep down that if I had heard him out, I would probably let things slide and succumb to his irresistible charm. It was better if I didn't see him.

"Not even 2 minutes?" he asked.

I didn't reply.

"C'mon Kate" he said. "I came all the way down here for you. You deserve to hear the truth. I really respect you, and... well, you know there's something happening between us. I'm just asking for a moment."

"Matt," I started. "Go home. Please. I'll think about it and get back to you."

"Well, okay Kate," he answered in a softer, more dejected tone. "I'm really sorry about everything. There's really a simple explanation, but I respect your request. I'll go now, but I want to leave this for you. I'm just sliding it under the door, okay? Please open it. Take care, Kate."

I didn't answer him. He slid a white, heavy stock envelope under the door. I heard him sigh, and listened to his steps as he walked away. Be strong, Kate. A part of me yearned for him. I was tempted to tear open the door and rush after him, so he could explain and I could forgive him. My stronger self would not allow me to do that. I picked up the envelope, and then walked back over to the sofa. I sat down for a few moments, trying to gather my thoughts, and my composure.

I noticed my breath had sped up from his visit. I was on edge, and he was back on my mind. It was partly the fight or flight reaction of having been awoken from sleep, and my mixed feelings about how I just handled myself. It was good ole' amygdala taking over, being primitive, as that part of the brain had been intended.

I never knew why certain lectures from my first year college psychology class would suddenly pop into my head at moments like this, but I ran with it. It was a beautifully analytical distraction from Matt. I thought about how the amygdala was made popular by that Seth guy. I couldn't remember his name. In any case, thinking about that part of the brain that controlled our survival instincts and ability to defend ourselves helped me to not think about Matt.

What else did I remember about the amygdala? It is fundamentally at the base of our emotional memory. What else? Yes, it's what causes us to fight, flee or freeze. And it makes us to act out trauma and protect any images we identified with during said trauma. I was trying to convince myself this was working.

What else did I remember about it? Oh yes. That small group of guys in psych class who would play out whole Star Wars scenes with their pens as laser swords, calling each other Padme Amidala or Padawan, to play on the professor's lecture. Men really could be such jokers. And I was fooling myself, if I thought that trying to distract myself with amygdala recall would get my mind off Matt. I sighed out loud.

I leaned back in the sofa and closed my eyes. Visions of him flooded into my consciousness and my breathing picked up again. I couldn't stop thinking about him, his touch, and how I felt around him. I reached over and picked up the envelope. Right away, I knew what it was before opening it.

My nana's necklace and pendant. How could I have forgotten it at his place? I must have left it in his room that night. I ripped open the envelope and started second guessing myself. Matt was so thoughtful to have gone looking through my burnt out unit to find it for me. How could I have not given him a second, to tell me what there was between him and Joy?

I began to feel I was being selfish and inconsiderate. No matter what he had to say, he deserved the opportunity to say it. Maybe I just didn't want to hear it, but that didn't mean I shouldn't give him that time. I decided I'd hear him out next time I saw him. If he hadn't completely give up on me already. I was pretty rude at the door earlier.

I hadn't been sitting on the sofa for more than 5 minutes since Matt left, when there was another round of knocking at the door. This time, it was more like banging and sounded aggressive. I wondered for a brief moment if it was Matt. Why would he come back like that? Maybe he thought he owned the place so he felt he could throw his weight around to get me to talk to him?

I decided I would open the door, and stick to my decision just moments earlier, to let him say his piece. Before I stood up, I heard a loud WHAM, like he was using his whole body weight to push against the door. The room was an L shape, so there was not a clear line of sight from the sofa to the front door. I sensed it had to be someone else.

"You don't need to do that," I shouted. Some fear was building inside me, so I didn't approach the door. "Are you looking for another hotel room? You can just go down to the front desk and ask them for help. I think you should just..."

Before I knew it, I heard a splintering crack, then a crash of the wooden door, as it gave way and fell. I couldn't believe that he would break the door down. I stepped back, looking around for something I could use to protect myself. There was only a vase, so I picked it up with both hands. I saw the shadow before the man, and that's when I knew with certainty that it was not Matt. The shadow was of a stout man, with long hair that met him at his shoulders.

"You're in the wrong room sir," I shouted, hoping he would leave.

He did not. He just stood there silently, out of my direct line of sight. Eventually, he said in a thick accent, "I here to make sure you no see nothing that night."

I was confused about his accent, but understood what he said. It didn't make sense, however that's when full-blown fear started to kick in for me. I didn't have anywhere to escape except to the adjoining room, so I turned around, looking at the door. There was barely any time to undo the latch. In my panic-filled haste, I fumbled with it, then heard him approaching behind me. I turned around and picked up the vase again.

"Get out!" I shouted.

"Listen girl," he said in a calm, but firm tone. "I only say this one time. You no see nothing in unit 16 that night. You understand?"

Unit 16? I had no idea what he was talking about, and I had never seen this man before. I screamed as loudly as I could, making a beeline around him to try and get out the same doorway he had just broken into. My shrill scream must have set him off, because he reached out and grabbed my shoulder. He quickly put one arm around my neck in a choke hold. My fighting instincts kicked in. Everything appeared to move in slow motion, and I vividly remember thinking to myself, "wow Kate, that was a timely lesson on the amygdala before this character broke down your door."

I stomped on his feet as hard as I could and threw one elbow back into his stomach area.

"Ouchhh!" he screeched. "You fucking bitch. I was just going to scare you little bit, but for that, now I fucking kill you!"

I squirmed, trying to get away, but he tightened his grip around my neck. I was stunned that he was here, choking me, let alone saying he'd kill me. It was surreal. I then reminded myself that I was in Manhattan, a large city, and this guy could be any mentally unstable person, or criminal for that matter.

I continued to struggle with him, but felt myself beginning to lose consciousness. I knew if I didn't do something right then, I would probably be done for. Had I let myself slip into unconsciousness, there would be no chance for me. What I had left in the way of strength was so very little, but I dug down deep and grabbed hold of possibility. Possible was better than dead. In that brief moment, I recalled my father telling me that if I was ever being attacked, go for the head and the eyes. I reached out with my hand that was still instinctively clenched around the vase, and crashed it against the wall beside us. As it shattered, I shoved the remaining piece left in my hand up and into his head.

He wailed, and loosened his grip enough for me to pull away. I stumbled forward, and bolted into the hallway to the elevator, pressing feverishly on the call button. I tried to scream to get the attention of anyone who could hear me, glancing back into the hallway to see if he was coming after me. Very little sound would come out, because of how hard he had choked me. And no one came.

~~ **GET BOOK 2 <u>HERE</u>** ~~
<u>www.amazon.com/dp/B00PYURJ50</u>

~~ ABOUT THE AUTHOR ~~

Bella Love-Wins writes contemporary romance and new adult & college stories based on my own deepest fantasies. The Billionaire Salvation Series is her first series, and shares some of her own imagined stories about the life and love of the wealthy. Bella is passionate about writing, and feels her talent is developing every day.

She is twenty -three years old and works as a communications analyst in a small firm. She lives a little north of Toronto and dreams of moving to the small town of Grimsby, Ontario one day. Bella would love to have a Shih Tzu and 2 cats as pets and practice kids. She enjoys running, snowboarding, and a good book – though not all at the same time.

Bella wrote her first short story at age 7, and has never stopped writing. She has always wanted to write, which is why she completed a degree in Communications and Literature. She dreams of improving her writing to where she can write fiction full time. Bella knows that it's with daily writing practice that she will improve. She has one older brother and her parents live in Northern Ontario.

A Word from Bella about her Stories

I find my stories to be about new adults and women in their mid-twenties, usually from wealthy families. This is because I went to school with the kids of some of the wealthiest families in Canada, and as I witnessed their woes first hand. My philosophy toward life is to believe that learning is possible, and that by learning every day, we can improve and grow. Thank you so much for checking out my stories at www.bellalovewins.com. Please enjoy one more sample of an upcoming story below, which is coming soon. It's called *Burnt*, Book One of The Wild Flames Series.

BURNT©

(A Complimentary Sample of the First Four Chapters)
Book One of The Wild Flames Series
(Copyright Bella Love-Wins, 2015 – All Rights Reserved)
Bella Love-Wins

Prologue

The four years of college were coming to an end and Tara Matthews couldn't believe that graduation was just a month away. She laid back on the couch, with her legs outstretched and covering Kevin Crawford's lap. They were best friends and had been since they were only five years old. The plan had always been that they would go to University of Alaska in Anchorage and then get their master's degree in Montana. They were so close to getting to Montana, Tara could feel it.

"What are you thinking about?" Kevin asked.

Their eyes locked, while she felt his hands massaging her feet that were still on his lap. "The past," she spoke nonchalantly. "We are about to leave Alaska. It just seems so surreal."

He smiled, nodding. "It does, but a new chapter in our lives is about to develop. That's exciting."

She had to admit that that was the truth. She had already started packing. She looked around his living room, knowing that it held many memories that she didn't want to give up. However, she knew that she was going to have another venture that would be filled with new memories. She felt his fingers kneading into her arches of her feet and she groaned. "God, you have the touch," she sighed, closing her eyes.

He laughed, "You sound so surprised," he replied, pressing his thumbs into the bottom of her feet. She smiled to herself. It was so comfortable with him and she didn't care who saw it. They had been through a lot of teasing growing up; where friends would point out that they should get together. Yet, Kevin and Tara both were persistent that the only thing between them was friendship. She didn't need to go out on other dates, because she could just be around Kevin and that was all she needed. It was uncomplicated.

She opened her eyes and saw that he was watching her. She smiled at him. "I probably should be going. It's getting late."

He ran his hands up and massaged her toes, one by one. "You could stay a little longer."

"I think you may have just talked me into it." She replied with a laugh, falling back to the couch and relaxing. She wasn't going anywhere.

+++

He looked in the window and glared at the couple on the couch. He wasn't couldn't hear what they were saying, but he knew that something was going on between them. "He's lied to me all this time." He said between clenched teeth.

He fought the urge to burst into that house and demand answers, but he held back. He couldn't let himself be seen...not yet. He needed to show her how much he cared about her first and always have. His eyes went to her feet and he watched as another man's hands slowly massaged her ankles. He was torn, not sure whether to look away or continue watching the interaction between them.

The smile on her face was breathtaking and an image that he would not be able to get out of his mind. He bit back a groan, fantasizing about her and hoping that one day she would be his. He turned from the window and went back to his rental car. He was going back to Washington State, so that he could devise his plan, but nothing and no one was going to get in his way.

Chapter 1

Three weeks later

Kevin stared at the transcript showing that he didn't pass his Advanced Zoology class. When he got the call to come into Dean Fredericks' office, he knew that couldn't be good. He took a deep breath and pushed through to the office. His secretary looked up and smiled. "Hello, how may I help you?"

"I...I need to see Dean Fredericks. He's expecting me. My name is Kevin Crawford." He stammered out the words, feeling his chest constrict. He hoped he didn't pass out from his anxiety.

"Sure. Have a seat and I will let him know that you are here." She picked up the phone as he took a seat. "There is a Mr. Crawford here to see you." He looked at her as she talked on her phone. She glanced at him and smiled again. He felt like a kid in the principal's office, getting ready to be punished for some woeful transgression. "I will let him know." She hung up the phone and turned to him. "He will be out in just a minute."

He nodded, picking up a magazine and pretending to read it. It was no use; he was reading the same line over and over again. When the door to Dean Frederick's office opened, he looked up and saw him coming out. "I'm ready for you," he said smoothly. Kevin put down the magazine and followed him to the office. He pointed to a chair and he took a seat, nervously looking around. "Thank you for coming in," he said. Kevin didn't feel he had much choice. "I take it you received your transcript."

Kevin looked down at the transcript and nodded. "I don't know what happened. I felt that I was doing well in that class, but...obviously not." The F stared back at him. He had always been a good student, so seeing that grade was something he would have never expected.

"It's not usually customary to call a student into my office. I am not here to be your babysitter or your father, but when I am forced to explain what happens next...I don't have much choice."

"What happens next?" Kevin asked. He knew what would happen next, he would have to retake the course and hold off on getting his Master's degree. It wasn't ideal, but he would make it work. He knew that was his only option if he wanted to further his degree.

"You were attending classes with a scholarship and that scholarship provided you student housing. I'm sorry to inform you that next year will not be covered with the scholarship. Since you didn't pass, the scholarship no longer takes care of those things." This was not something Kevin had thought about. The realization of what the Dean had intonated began to sink in. He was staying in the houses on campus and that was going to end. "You will need to find housing off campus," Dean Frederick paused before continuing, "you can also take the online course, but it's up to you."

Kevin groaned. Things were just getting more and more dire. "I understand," he said. He had been working diligently to gain a career that interested him and he wouldn't give up on that. He stood up and shook his hand. "Thank you," he replied, even though his mind was reeling with what was going to happen the following year.

He left the building in a daze, walking back to his car. He didn't know where he was going, but he knew that he didn't want to go back to his lonely place. He began driving, until he finally stopped in front of Tara's apartment. He knew that if anyone could make him feel better, it was her.

+++

Tara loaded up another box of her belongings. Her roommate had already finished up and was out with her boyfriend, so that they could say their goodbyes. Tara was glad to have the house to herself. She enjoyed having a little time alone.

As she was closing up another box, she heard a knock on her door. "Coming," she called, getting up and heading to the door. She peeked through the peephole to find Kevin standing outside. She quickly opened the door. "I am so glad you're here. You can help me pack," she laughed, as he walked in. "I'm about done, but I have a few more things to go." She looked back at him and he smiled a little. "You know me...I tend to be a hoarder." She paused, glancing around the living room. "I am going to miss this place. It has been nice living here." She turned to him. "We graduate in a week...a week," she shook her head, glancing at him, "can you believe that?"

He let out an uncomfortable groan. That was the first time she stopped to see that he didn't appear as happy as she was. In fact, she saw sadness in his eyes. Their eyes connected for a moment. "So, what do you need help with?" He asked, brushing past her.

She reached out and touched his arm, stopping him. "It can wait. What's wrong?"

He seemed nervous, as he shifted from one foot to the other, but then suddenly stopped. "I won't be graduating when you do, Tara." The words came out hurriedly and she almost wondered if she heard them correctly.

She stared at him, sure that she misunderstood what he was saying. "Right," she chuckled. She realized that he wasn't laughing, which was something that she had expected him do, once he confessed that he was only teasing. He wouldn't even look her in her eyes. "Kevin, look at me." When he looked up, she saw that he wasn't kidding. He looked ashamed, and that alarmed her. "What are you talking about?"

He looked away for a moment, like he was gathering his thoughts, but then faced her again. "I flunked Advanced Zoology."

Her face fell, as she processed the words. "But how?"

"I don't know what happened," he answered. "I studied. But somehow, I flunked the exam and that brought my final grade down. I have to take it again for chance to get into the Master's program. So I won't be graduating with you and there is nothing I can do to change that."

She felt a pit in her stomach. The dream always was to continue their education together. They both had the same aspirations and so it only made sense that they would follow them as a team. She didn't know how she could do it alone. She walked over to him and placed her hand on his shoulder. "I'm sorry, Kevin." She needed to console him, because she knew that he would be by her side if the situations were reversed. "You won't have to do this alone."

He turned his head, so that he was looking at her. She noticed his brown eyes had darkened. They had a hint of gold in them that seemed to brighten or darken depending on his mood. She stepped back, noticing the intensity of his stare. "How do you figure?" he asked, raising an eyebrow. "You'll be in Montana, pursuing everything you've worked hard for," he paused, "and you should."

A thousand thoughts were running through her mind, none of them in any way cohesive. She finally looked up at him, "I'm not going anywhere." She said, noticing the immediate shock on his face. "We have been a team and when one team member is down, the other one helps him through. Montana can wait."

"I can't let you do that, Tara. This team member is not about to ask his best friend to stay behind."

She shook her head, "You're not asking. I'm telling you. I want to do this." She swallowed the lump in her throat. She was onboard with her decision, but the fact of the matter was she was a little disappointed. She couldn't deny that.

"Are you sure?" he asked. "I don't want you to feel obligated to stay, when you've worked so hard."

Tara shook her head, "Will you stop saying that I have worked hard. We've both worked hard and I'm going to help you ace this course next time." She smiled, "That's what friends are for." She moved past him, hoping that he couldn't see the conflict probably playing out on her face. "Now, help me pack up. We still can't stay here, so we might as well go back to Washington State. I'm sure our parents will love to see us," she spoke the words with mild sarcasm. Both their parents had given them free reign to run, barely there when they were growing up.

She felt him brushing up against her and she looked up into his eyes. "I'm going to ask you one more time. Are you positive that this is what you want to do? I won't be upset if you choose to go to Montana. I swear."

"Kevin, I couldn't imagine going to Montana without you. It's just the way it is. I promise you that I want to do this. I wouldn't have said it otherwise." She turned back to her boxes and continued to pack. She felt at peace. She knew she made the right choice. She was positive he'd do the same for her. More than anything, she wanted to keep their friendship intact and if this was what she needed to do, then she was going to do it.

+++

"Tara Matthews!" Kevin cheered as her name was called. He caught a glimpse of her as she walked across that stage. Admittedly, there was a palpable pang of regret he felt inside. He wasn't up there with her, but that disappeared as she turned her tassel.

He still couldn't believe that she was making the sacrifice for him. He would have never expected that and he still didn't know how he felt about it. He tried to focus on the rest of the graduation, but his mind wandered back to the day that they made the decision to go to University of Alaska.

"I chose the school that I am going to attend," she announced proudly. He stood there, knowing that he had been waiting for this day. He would have gone anywhere that she decided. "University of Alaska."

He nearly choked on the pizza he was eating. "Alaska?" he asked, snickering. "Could you have chosen anywhere colder?" He was being sarcastic, but a part of him was excited about the new adventure. He had never been to Alaska before.

She shrugged, "It has the best program for Wildlife Preservation."

He cringed, "I know, but Alaska..." he shivered, "I get cold just thinking about it."

She rolled her eyes, "What does it matter to you. It's not like you are going. I'm the one going."

He couldn't believe she didn't know that he had every intention of following her. Even if they both swore they would never be anything more than friends, he still wanted to be near her. She was the one person that understood him and he didn't want to give that up. "You aren't planning on going alone, are you?" he asked with slight hesitation.

"Well, I thought that that's the way that things usually worked. When you go away to college, it tends to mean that you're going away from everything that's familiar, to expand your horizons and get out of your comfort zone." She paused, "Doesn't it?"

He laughed, "Usually, but we don't have a usual relationship. I have every intention of tagging along. Unless, you would rather I didn't. You might think it could hinder your chances of meeting someone, if they think that there's something going on between us."

She playfully pushed him and started laughing. "Like I have ever worried about that before." She stood there, with a smile crossing her lips. Her blue eyes were shining and her long, wavy brown hair was pulled into an over the shoulder ponytail. "I can't even imagine what it would be like without you there." She threw her arms around him and he held her close. He could feel her breath against his skin. He took in the smell of jasmine that she was wearing in her perfume. "I would love for us to go together."

He opened his eyes just as the audience was standing to their feet to applaud the entire graduating class. He stood up and joined in. He was so proud of her. As they filed out of the auditorium, he looked around for her. She found him first and greeted him with a smile and a hug. "You did it," he said, trying to push away all the negativity he was feeling for himself.

She pulled back, still holding onto her smile. "Now, it's your turn. Are you ready to go home?"

He looked around the auditorium of their campus, knowing that he would be back. "I'm ready," he looped his arm through hers and they headed out of the building. They were packed and ready to go back to Washington State. He knew that with her support, he would be able to make both their dreams a reality.

Chapter 2

Tara said goodbye to Kevin and walked into her parents' home. He had helped her bring some of her things to the garage, and the rest of the boxes to the porch, and then left. She was alone to face her parents, which is how she wanted it. She looked around the foyer, which brought back old memories. "Hello?" She called out.

After several minutes, she heard footsteps. Her mom entered the room. "Hi Tara, I didn't know you were going to be here." Her mom kissed her on the cheek.

"Yeah, after graduation I figured that I would come home until I go back."

"Go back?" She asked, cocking her head. "Once you graduate, don't you go forward?"

Tara rolled her eyes, but looked away from her mother's expectant gaze. She had been practicing this conversation ever since she made the decision to take a year off. She wanted to say that she couldn't believe her mom would care, when she didn't even bother to come to the graduation. However, she thought against that. "I decided to take a year off before going to Montana." Her mom just stared at her, not saying a word, so she continued. "I have a lot that I want to do and I feel a year would do me some good." She didn't feel she could tell the truth, but she had to admit that the excuse she gave sounded lame.

"Oh..." her mother slowly spoke. "So, are you staying home until you discover yourself?" she asked with deep sarcasm etched in her voice.

"I'll try not to stay any longer than I have to, mom" Tara replied. "Now, if you'll excuse me...I have some boxes to grab," she mumbled, as she turned on her heels and left the house. She went to the porch, fighting every urge to run to her car and drive away. She took moved the bigger boxes into to the garage, where she would store most of her things.

She paused, before heading back to the porch. She only had her mother to deal with. Kevin had his parents and his brother. She hoped he was doing better than she was.

+++

Kevin tried the doorknob, before realizing that it was locked. He had searched to find his old house key but had no luck. He had to knock. He knocked once and then twice, before trying a third time. Finally, on the third attempt, he heard footsteps. When the door opened, it was his father he saw standing there.

His dad's face had a mixture of emotions, but then he put out his hand and they shook hands. "Hello, son. This is a surprise." Kevin entered the house. "What are you doing here?"

"Can't a guy come home without a lot of questions?" he asked, hoping it didn't come across as rude. He let out a breath and tried to put a smile on his lips. "I have had a couple of crazy weeks," he replied, using it as an excuse. He looked around, "Where's Mom and Jake?"

"Your mother went to the grocery store and Jake...well who knows where he is."

He frowned at the last comment, but he wasn't surprised. The family all believed his eighteen year old brother had Schizophrenia and from some of the stories, it was possible. However, Kevin chose to look past it and hope that they were all wrong, but was willing to help him through it if they were right. "Do you mind if I stay here in my old room?"

"For how long?" his dad asked.

Kevin shrugged, "Until I can find another alternative." He wanted to argue that it shouldn't matter if he was there or not.

After all, he was sure his parents could go about their everyday activities even if he was there. It never bothered them before.

His dad raised his eyebrow. "Do you need to tell me something?" Kevin shook his head slowly. "Aren't you going to Montana in a couple of weeks?" he was asked.

Kevin knew that eventually it would all come out anyway. "I won't be going to Montana," he replied. "At least not for another year." He grimaced at the thought of telling the whole truth, so he just blurted it out. "I flunked a class and have to retake it next semester." There was a long pause, before a word was said. "Say something, dad," Kevin replied.

"I am speechless. Was it because you spent a lot of time partying?" he finally asked him.

Kevin's jaw dropped, "What? No...I studied, but apparently it wasn't enough. I don't know what happened, but this summer I am going to spend studying and when I go back...I will work harder." He wanted it to be true, but there were no guarantees.

"Well, good luck with that." The snide remark came from his dad.

He didn't expect much support, but he also didn't expect that after a year of not seeing each other, that his dad would be so distant. He just hoped that things between his mom and brother were better. He didn't know how much of this he could take.

+++

Kevin and Tara immediately got down to studying so that he could be ready to pass the course with flying colors this time. That way, they could go back to their original plan. It was also a way to find an escape. They found various places to study, from her place, to his, to the local diner, and the library. They changed it up a lot.

Tara's favorite place to help him study was at her place. Most of the time, it was just the two of them and no interruptions. That evening, Kevin was due to arrive for another study session at her house. As she waited, lay on the couch and watched the local news.

"Just outside of Richard's Bakery today, a body was discovered in the dumpster."

She perked up. She had worked at Richard's Bakery when she was a junior in high school.

"The body was set on fire and has not yet been identified. Officials at the Coroner's office have confirmed they are awaiting dental records for the purpose of identification of the victim. At this time, the death is considered as suspicious; however no suspects have been detained. This is the second body that has been found just this week, leaving the police to wonder if they're related. We will continue to monitor this story and keeping you informed of any updates as they come in."

Tara heard the doorbell, so she muted the television. She was expecting Kevin, so she moved briskly to the door and opened it up.

"Hello," Kevin said as he walked in.

"Hey." She closed the door and turned back to him. He was looking around and she knew what he was looking for. "We're alone. My mom had some kind of meeting tonight. She said she will probably be late."

He seemed to sigh with relief. "That's not what I was looking for."

She laughed, "Sure it wasn't."

They went into the living room and she picked up the remote control to shut the television off. "Did you hear about the body they found in the dumpster at Richard's Bakery?"

"Yeah. It's the second death." He put his books down and sat down on the couch. "It's unusual for this small town."

Tara shook her head and sat next to him. "It's sad it has come to this."

Kevin nodded with agreement. He opened his book and hesitated before flipping to the chapter they had planned to work on that week. He looked up and met her stare, "I just want to thank you again for what you did, and for all your help. I couldn't do it without you."

She smiled, "You don't need to keep thanking me. Besides, it lets me catch up on my knitting." She laughed as she picked up her next project. She was working on another winter hat. "So, taking some time off will allow me to get some things done." She meant what she said. She really was enjoying the much needed rest. "I have been thinking lately."

"About what?" he asked.

"Well...I really would like to get out of here. My mom's here alone and still, she acts like I'm not welcomed. I never understood why she treats me this way. In any case, I was thinking about finding a part-time job, saving up some money, and looking for another temporary place to stay."

"That might not be such a bad idea," he replied, agreeing with her. "My folks are being the same way, which makes no sense as Jake is still at home. I could use some extra money too."

She smiled, "Well, then let's make it our mission to find a summer job." She thought about it and got excited, "We're still ahead of the high school students, so we have a good chance of finding work. Maybe we could even find something that'll look good on a resume for the future." She pointed to his books, "For now...let's get back to studying."

He flipped the pages to the next chapter and they began to work. She knitted while he read and took notes on index cards. It was easy and their study routine was forming. Everything was going perfectly.

+++

Tara held up another notecard and he rattled off the information on the animal. Kevin was getting quicker in his response time. His confidence was growing too. He began to believe he could get through the exam with better results. "How about this one?" She said through a yawn.

He chuckled. "That is a bandicoot. It is a marsupial that is mainly found in Australia. It is a nocturnal animal and during the daytime it seeks out shelter in bush land areas."

She nodded, yawning again. "Very good."

He laughed, "Well, you're obviously tired." He looked at his watch and realized they had been studying for nearly four hours. "I should get going. It's late and we both could use a break."

She smiled, "You're probably right." She reached over to the coffee table and grabbed the hat she had knitted. "At least take this with you," she snickered and handed it over to him. It wasn't the first item she had knitted for him, but he would never get tired of receiving one of her homemade creations.

"Thank you!" He put it on, "How do I look?" He held out his arms, looking away and standing up.

She laughed. "Lookin' good," she replied, causing him to look at her. "I have to say; we made pretty good progress today."

Kevin loved the sound of her laughter. He fought the urge to reach out and brush her hair behind her shoulder, nodding instead and walking toward the door. "We make a good team," he said, turning to her.

She smiled, "Always have." He knew that that was the truth. It was also why he never felt the need to go out with other girls, because she was always there. "Goodnight, Kevin." As they remained at the door, with neither moving, he saw her leaning up to kiss his cheek.

Kevin turned his face, caused their lips to connect. As her body leaned into his, he went to wrap his arms around her, but the kiss ended all too soon. She opened her mouth to speak, but it was like she had no words. She covered her mouth and looked away from him. "I..." he began.

"My aim never was too good," she replied. Her face was red.

He shook his head, "It was my fault. I got caught up in the moment. It's late and I didn't mean to make things awkward."

"You didn't," she quickly said. "It's just that I was caught a little off guard. That's all."

He stepped back and reached for the doorknob. He could tell that she was confused, by the look in her eyes and he didn't want to make things even more complicated by staying. "I'd better be going," he replied.

He stepped out onto the porch. She lifted her hand and waved, while he headed back to his car. He got inside, but couldn't bring himself to leave. He turned to look at her through his window. She remained in the doorway, like a statue. He slowly turned and put his car into drive, leaving the front of her house. He wasn't sorry that he kissed her, but he would not push her. He knew that it would only confuse the situation and the last thing he wanted to do was make her uncomfortable.

Chapter 3

Tara couldn't stop thinking about the kiss. No matter how hard she tried, thoughts of his lips on hers would come rushing back in. She tried to focus on television, reading, sleeping, and even internet surfing, but nothing was working.

After a few days, as she was looking over job postings on the internet, he phoned her. She hadn't talked to him since their last study session and she was almost apprehensive answering the phone. *What if he wants to discuss it?* She thought to herself. She wiped her sweaty palms on her shorts and answered her cellphone. "Hello?" She hoped that she didn't sound strange, but she feared he would be able to hear her uneasiness.

"Hey, it's me. What are you doing right now?"

She glanced back at the computer, hitting dead end after dead end of job prospects. "Nothing much."

"Good. Get dressed. Put on something that looks like business casual and I'll pick you up in twenty minutes."

"Wh..." her words trailed off, when she realized that he had already hung up. She groaned, pulling herself from the kitchen table. She could only imagine what she was getting herself into. She went upstairs and headed to her bedroom, where she pulled out a khaki pair of pants and a short-sleeved red blouse from her closet.

She quickly got dressed and brushed her hair. As she left her bedroom, she called out to her mom. "I'm going out. Don't know when I will be back."

She didn't hear anything in response, so she shrugged and headed downstairs. She peeked outside to see that Kevin was already there and he was leaning on the hood of his car. She paused to stare at him for a moment. He looked well put together, with his brown shaggy hair perfectly in place. She rarely saw him dressed up, as after the kiss, she looked at him in a different light. She tried to shake the thought out of her mind, grabbed her purse, and headed outside.

He stood up, watching her as she headed down the front walkway. "So, what's going on?" she asked.

He opened up the door for her and waited for her to get in. "I have a surprise for you and I don't want to ruin it by telling you. You'll find out soon enough."

She was hesitant about flying blind, but figured she could trust him. She got into the passenger seat and waited for him to join her. As she looked at him, the smile had never left his lips. Whatever he was doing was something that he seemed very proud of. She couldn't deny she was excited to find out what it was.

+++

They drove toward their destination and Kevin was relieved that she didn't question him more. He had hoped she would be as excited over it as he was. He looked at her from the corner of his eye. Thoughts of how he had wrapped his arms around her and pulled her close when he stole that kiss came flooding back into his mind. He cursed at himself for getting caught up in it. It was just a silly kiss. It probably meant nothing to her, so to dwell on it was stupid.

"Are you sure you don't want to tell me where we're going?" she asked.

"I'm positive," he laughed. "We'll be there in another five minutes. You can wait that long, right?"

"If I have to," She chuckled, glancing back out the window. When five minutes passed, he pulled into a parking lot.

"I don't understand." She spoke, as they parked near the main entrance of the petting zoo. "What are we doing here?"

He smiled, "Look..." he pointed his finger to a sign by the front door.

She turned and read it out loud. "Now hiring! Interviews at 2:00."

He looked at his watch. "We're early."

"I've been looking online for the past three days for a job. This could be perfect." She seemed optimistic and he was thrilled about that.

He had to agree. They both loved animals, wildlife, and being around people. The local petting zoo was the best choice for them. He noticed Tara frowning and wondered why she was down. "What are you thinking about?" he asked softly.

She turned to face him and he thought that she was going to explain. Instead she shook her head, "It's nothing. We'd better get in there."

For a moment he considered asking her again if something was bothering her. He had a feeling that he was missing something, but as their eyes met he decided to ignore his gut feeling. They got out of the car and headed up to the door, where he opened it for her to enter first. He looked around the entrance. At least fifteen other people were standing around. "I wonder how many they are hiring," he whispered to her.

She stopped abruptly, causing him to run into her. "That's what I'm worried about," she replied, turning around. They were inches from one another. Her breath was shallow. Her eyes widened as she stepped backward. "Wh...What if..." she let out a breath. "Let me try this again...what if only one of us gets a job?"

He scrunched up his nose. He hadn't given that possibility any thought. They did everything together, so this would be just one more thing to add to their list. As Kevin thought about her fear, he knew that it wouldn't matter to him if she got a job and he didn't. "How would you feel if I got a job and you didn't?" he asked, trying to gauge her response before she spoke.

She opened her mouth, but then quickly shut it.

"If you are worried about it, then you must have thought about it," he said, gently trying to nudge her along and hear her answer.

She turned to look at the growing group of applicants, and then resumed looking at him. "It wouldn't matter to me. I would be happy for you."

He smiled, "Same here, so we have nothing to worry about. Agreed?"

After a moment of her contemplating that idea, she smiled. "Agreed."

He went to the front desk, where she followed him. They each grabbed an application and found a place to sit down. They read over the forms and tediously filled theirs out. Although it didn't matter to him, a part of him did hope that they would each get a job there and he was sure that Tara felt the same way.

+++

The interview process was painless. She figured it had to be kept short, because there were still five people waiting for their chance. When she left his office, she walked out into the entrance, where Kevin was sitting waiting for her. He looked up and stood to greet her. "How did it go?"

"I think overall it was fine. They said that if I make the cut, then I will hear something by tomorrow. At least we don't have to wait too long to get an answer." They walked out of the building and headed to his car. "They also said that there are only three positions available and there were twenty-four applicants." She stopped, as he held the door open for her. "Our chances aren't great."

"It might seem like a longshot, but I have reason to believe that we both would make a great addition to this team." He winked at her and she rolled her eyes. "What? You don't believe that?"

"What we believe and what will actually happen are two completely different things."

"You know what? I know just what you need," he replied.

"Oh yeah? What's that?" she asked.

"A nice hot meal from Marmalade's. It's been a long time."

She didn't know if food would do the trick, but she was willing to give it a try, especially when it had been a long time since she had had one of their chocolate cheesecake desserts. "You talked me into it. It won't get rid of this doubt, but this couldn't hurt."

He laughed, and as they headed toward Marmalade's, she had already begun to relax. If it wasn't meant to be, then it wasn't. That was the motto she felt they needed to adopt when it came to summer jobs.

They pulled into the parking lot of the restaurant and Kevin parked close to the main entrance. As they got out of the car and headed up to the door, it felt like they were on a real date.

"After you," Kevin said, as he held the door open for her.

"Thank you," she replied.

They headed up to the hostess podium and as it was before dinner hour, they were seated almost instantly. Neither of them bothered to look at the menu. The waitress arrived quickly and they each chose the lasagna. When the waitress left, their conversation flowed easily.

"You know," Kevin starter, "I have been thinking a lot lately about how our friendship started."

Tara frowned, "You have? I don't even think I remember." It wasn't the truth. She could picture it to a tee, but she wasn't about to confess at all. She found herself thinking about it regularly as well, because the way they ended up becoming friends was a shocker to most.

He cocked his head. "You have to be kidding me. Don't you remember how you socked a snowball at me for no apparent reason?"

She put her hands on her hips, "Kevin Crawford, you know very well that I had plenty of reason. We were in Kindergarten and you said my snowsuit was weird."

He raised an eyebrow and took a drink of his water. "I thought you said you didn't remember?" he laughed.

She knew that he was trying to get a rise out of her and it was working. She playfully threw a napkin at him for teasing her. "Fine...maybe I remember it a little bit," she replied with a laugh. "The bottom line is, I must have been caught by your charm, because we have been friends ever since." He smiled warmly. "It does make me wonder what the defining reason was that made our friendship so strong."

"We're so much alike," she replied nonchalantly. "We both came from families that were distant and we needed someone who would understand us. I feel we were that person for each other. I don't know anyone that gets me more than you do."

"Or vice versa," he agreed. He looked down at his water glass. "There is something else that I wanted to discuss with you."

Tara could tell that whatever he wanted to talk about, it would be deep. Looking over at him, he seemed to have the weight of the world on his shoulders. She felt a pang of urgency to change the subject. She had a feeling that his sudden change of mood was because he was thinking about their kiss. That was another thing that bonded their friendship, the ability to read one another's mind. "Kevin, don't..." she began, but her words were broken off when she saw that their food was heading their way. "Thank you," she mumbled, as the waitress put their food down.

"Need anything else?" she asked them.

Tara glanced at Kevin and he was staring at her. "No, but thank you," she answered.

The waitress walked away and he resumed the conversation.

"Tara, we need to discuss it."

"We already did," she begged for him to drop it. "It just happened and that's all there is to it. I don't want things to make this awkward between us."

"I..." he started. "I am relieved to hear you say that."

"You are?" she asked, surprised.

"I am," he stated. "I don't want anything to get in way of our friendship and I just wanted to make sure that you felt the same way."

She looked down at her food. It was what she wanted, but there was something nagging at her mind and telling her that something was missing. She looked up and put a smile on, "Great!" She took a bite of her food, and he did the same.

Their meal was interrupted when his phone rang. She turned her attention on him. He glanced down at the caller ID and shrugged. "I better answer it. Hello?" he paused and his eyes went to hers. "Yes, this is Kevin Crawford." His eyes got big. "That's great news." He hesitated for a moment, then spoke up. "What about Tara Matthews?" His face fell, "Oh...I understand. Thank you."

When he disconnected the call, Tara knew what it was about. "You got the job?"

He nodded, "Yeah. I asked about you and..."

"I didn't get it," Tara replied, feeling jealousy welling up inside of her. "That's alright. I told you that I wouldn't be upset if I didn't get it. I am happy for you."

"Well, I don't know if you got it or not. They wouldn't tell me."

"Oh..." she felt a sudden breath of air escape her. That was better than a no. She took a drink, clearing the lump in her throat. A chance was good. She tried to go back to eating her meal, but her thoughts kept roaming back to her phone and the fact that no one had called yet.

When they were finished with their main course and ordering their dessert, she was past losing all hope. She at least expected a call to tell her that she didn't get a job, but she knew that rejection calls would probably come later. They had been told that they could be called back as late as the next day, so she wasn't going to lose all hope. Not yet anyway.

Their desserts came and she let it whisk her away. She ate slowly, moaning between bites, and relishing the taste. She sighed as the last piece was gone. "That does take away a lot of problems."

He laughed. "Yes, it does. You know, I don't have to take the job," he suddenly said.

She turned to him, "Yes...you do. I'll be fine no matter what happens. I..." her words were cut off when her phone started ringing. She grabbed it out of her purse and found a number that she didn't recognize. She answered the call. "Hello?"

"Hello, is this Tara Matthews?"

"Yes..." she quietly answered, silently crossing her fingers.

"Hello, Ms. Matthews. This is Zoe from Baker Street Petting Zoo. We were very impressed by your interview and we would like to offer you a job."

She met his waiting stare and just nodded. He smiled at her. "Thank you so much. I graciously accept and I appreciate you calling me. Goodbye," she disconnected the call and sighed with relief. Another plan was working out and she knew it would only bring good things.

+++

Across from the restaurant, he watched them. He couldn't hear what they were saying, but he felt he could read their body language. She was smiling at him and he was looking lovingly at her. They were playing with his mind. Through the main course and into dessert, they were acting like they were a couple. They weren't supposed to be a couple.

He saw the waitress approach them to pick up their finished plates. For a moment, his attention shifted to the waitress as she left the table. When he looked back at Kevin and Tara, they were leaving the restaurant, laughing and enjoying themselves. He got up, sick to his stomach that she could betray him so blatantly. They couldn't get away with this for much longer. For the moment, he decided to keep following them, knowing that one day soon, they would both realize what a huge mistake they were making.

Chapter 4

Tara walked out of the building and saw Kevin feeding a goat with a bottle. They had been working at the petting zoo for two weeks and she was enjoying the job. She could tell that Kevin was, too. She even noticed that their friendship seemed to be growing and she had not thought it was possible. They were already so close. She approached him, just watching. He must have sensed her presence, because he looked up and smiled. "Hey!"

She nodded to greet him and glanced around the yard. There were horses, pigs, goats, and even a dog and cat that graced the backyard. The smaller animals, like chickens, rabbits, and guinea pigs, were inside. She looked back at him. He was feeding the baby goat with a small bottle. "Now I know how you'll look when you become a father," she teased.

He laughed, "It might be a little bit different."

She snickered, "Maybe a little." She cleared her throat before continuing. "I came out here for a reason. Mr. Harrison is ready to do your two week evaluation."

"Oh great," he laughed. "It was nice working with you."

She shook her head, "I already had mine. It wasn't bad. It's more along the lines of, is the job working out for you...things like that. As long as you don't have any issues, then you should be in there about five minutes." She looked at the goat, which still had a half of bottle to go. "I can take over."

"Are you sure?" he teased. "It's a pretty tough job."

"I think that I can handle it, Kevin, but thanks for asking."

He smiled, winking at her and handing over the bottle. She took over the rest of the feeding and looked at him as he headed up to the building, then disappeared through the door. She chuckled, turning back to the goat. "It's just you and me kid," she replied, laughing to herself.

She didn't realize she wasn't alone, until she heard talking behind her.

"You both make a cute couple." It was Amy Watters, the third person who had won the summer job.

She laughed, "Oh...we're not a couple." She looked down at the goat, ignoring the fact that Amy was still standing there.

"Huh..." she heard her say. "I must admit, that does surprise me. Are you being serious right now?"

Tara looked up and nodded, "Yeah, Kevin and I go way back. We're just good friends." As she said the words, even she noticed how different they sounded to her. She had been denying accusations that something was going on between them for years. Normally she would laugh it off. This time, she felt a pang of regret for saying it.

"Wow...so you won't mind if I go out with him?"

Tara had turned to walk to leave the animal enclosure, but as she heard the question, she flipped her head back to stare at Amy. She fumbled for words and they weren't there. It was too late to retract her earlier statement. She could only shrug. "Of course not. If Kevin and you want to go out, you don't need my permission."

Amy was visibly excited. "Great. Thank you, Tara."

Tara left the goat's enclosure, in a daze. She had just given Amy permission to take away her closest friend.

+++

Kevin's evaluation went just like Tara had said it would. There was nothing to worry about. He headed out the manager's office and saw that Tara had moved on from the goat and was sweeping out a horse's stall. He heading toward her, but Amy cut across the hallway and stopped him.

"So, did you have your evaluation?" she asked.

He nodded, "Just coming from it. You?"

"Yep." She replied casually. She then looked around, fidgeting nervously. "Got a minute? I wanted to ask you something."

"Okay..." he crossed his arms in front of him. "I'm listening."

She got straight to the point. "I was wondering if you'd like to go out some time."

Kevin hadn't expected that. She seemed nice and all, but had never approached him much to get to know him before. She also did not appear to be someone that would ask a guy out.

"You mean like a date?" he asked, glancing over at where Tara was still working. He pulled himself back to the woman standing in front of him. "Is that what you mean?"

"Yes," she replied, again looking nervous. "Unless you have some reason why you can't go out. Like...you're dating someone else." She hesitated and turned toward Tara, then glanced back at him. "Are you?"

He quickly shook his head. "No...I'm not."

"Okay," she let out a breath. "That's what Tara said, but I thought that maybe she was kidding."

He nodded, "You talked to Tara about it?"

She nodded, "I honestly thought you were both dating each other, but she set me straight."

The words settled in and he knew the truth behind them. She didn't want to date him and at some point he was going to have to recognize that. "We're just friends. How about after work today? Tara drove me, but if you wouldn't mind taking me home afterward..." his words dropped off.

She smiled, shaking her head. "Not at all. After work sounds great."

"Great," he replied. "Speaking of work, we better get back to it," he replied. "See you later."

He winked at her, knowing that he was flirting, but was also hurt by Tara's eagerness to pass him off to someone else. He tried to forget about it as he stepped into the stable next to the one Tara was working in. He didn't greet her or make eye contact as he raked the hay.

Tara noticed him and cleared her throat to get his attention.

"Yes?" he asked, sounding annoyed.

She cocked her head, frowning, but didn't say anything at first.

"What, Tara?" he said impatiently.

"How did your evaluation go?" she asked.

"Fine...just like you said it would," he replied, turning back to his work. "Oh...by the way, I just wanted to let you know that I won't need a ride home."

"You won't?" she sounded confused.

He looked up again and shook his head, "I have a date and she's going to take me home."

The color left Tara's face. There was no denying it now. "Oh. I hope you have a great time." She looked over to him. "Amy?" She asked.

He nodded, "She said you two had a nice chat."

She shrugged, "She thought we were dating. I let her know we were just great friends. Apparently, it's a good thing I did. You two have a date, and I am sure you'll both be extremely happy with each other." Tara turned on her heels and headed back to the corner of her stall.

Kevin couldn't help but laugh.

"What's so funny?" she asked, looking at him with a mixture of sarcasm and anger.

"You seem jealous," he raised an eyebrow.

She glared at him, "I am not jealous. I'm simply wishing you well."

She stared at him, waiting for him to say something else about it. He knew that it would not be wise to provoke her more, so he went back to working. He held onto the hope that she wasn't being honest with him and that she really was jealous. It held a certain appeal about it.

They finished off with work few hours later. As Kevin stood outside waiting leave for his date with Amy, he caught sight of Tara leaving the building.

"Hey," he said.

"Hey," she replied. They hadn't talked much after their conversation in the horses' stalls. He wanted to make sure that they were still on good terms.

"I'll see you tomorrow night, right?"

She paused, "Tomorrow night?"

He nodded, "Our movie night. It's Saturday," he spoke. They had a ritual that they had started in college. Every first Saturday of the month they would go to the movies, alternating on who got to pick the show that month. "It's your pick, remember?"

"Oh. Well let's play it by ear." She said, moving past him.

He stopped her before she could reach her car. "Play it by ear?" he asked. "Come on, Tara. You don't want to break tradition, do you?"

She turned and looked at him. Her eyes looked past his shoulder. "Your ride's ready." She replied, motioning with her head. "We'll talk later." She turned back to her car and left as soon as she could.

Kevin watched her pull out of the parking spot. He felt like a part of him was going with her. He slowly turned around and saw that Amy was leaning up against her car, waiting patiently for him.

He walked back to her and smiled, "Sorry about that."

"Lover's spat?" she asked.

He opened his mouth. "No, we told you that—"

"I'm teasing," she replied with a laugh. "Get in. I'm starved." She opened up her car door and he got in the passenger side. He looked out the window and could only think about Tara.

Everything had better work out, he thought. He hated feeling like he was betraying her.

As they drove to the restaurant, he heard Amy talking, but could barely think about anything else. "So, you decided not to go to school?" he asked, trying to keep up the conversation.

"I decided to take some time off. I hated high school and I figured that if I despised going to school that much, then how could I possibly get interested in college courses?" From her tone he could tell that she was a couple of years younger than he was or at least seemed like it. "You've taken college courses, correct?" she asked. He nodded, as she pulled into the parking lot of a small Italian restaurant.

They got out of the car and headed up to the front door. As he held the door open for Amy, she beamed. He was less excited by the minute. "Two please..." he called to the hostess. After a ten minute wait, they were directed to a table for two at the window.

Amy continued as soon as they sat down. "So you're done college?"

"Yes," he answered. "I have one more course until I complete my Bachelor's degree with University of Alaska. I plan on going to Montana to work on my Masters after," he smiled.

She looked impressed. "That's awesome. I wish you the best," she replied, looking down at the menu.

They perused their menus for a while, then placed their order and resumed their discussion of dreams and ambitions. Amy was satisfied living in their small town and working at the petting zoo. She had no future plans, and there was nothing wrong with that, but Kevin quickly realized he had little in common with her. He could tell that she felt the same way too. There was no romantic spark between them.

"Are you being honest when you say you and Tara are just friends?" she asked, taking a drink.

He looked up. He didn't expect she would be that direct during their date. He nodded. "Yes, Tara and I have always been friends."

"Yet, you want more," she stated it with confidence.

He shook his head, laughing. "Why would you say that?"

She rolled her eyes, "Call it women's intuition," she shrugged. "Or, you can call it just a hunch. Either way, I am sure that I haven't missed the signs. I think you two would make a great couple."

Their meals arrived and their conversation remained friendly and light. He did enjoy their discussion, and it felt good to finally have someone he could be honest with about his feelings for Tara. "You realize this conversation has to stay between us, right?" he said.

She laughed. "Your secret is safe with me, but one day you might want to tell her. Things could be better then."

He wasn't sure about that, but nodded. After finishing up their meals, Kevin placed some cash on the table to pay their bill, resisting her insistence that she should pay. "It doesn't matter that you invited me. I want to pay," he told her. She reluctantly agreed.

They were about to head out when he saw Jake heading their way. "Hey, I didn't expect to see you here." Jake said, looking between Kevin and Amy.

The feeling was mutual. Kevin noticed the Amy's confusion on her face, as there was a clear resemblance between him and Jake. "Amy, this is my brother, Jake. Jake, this is my co-worker, Amy."

"Nice to meet you," Amy said, sticking out her hand.

"Likewise," Jake said, smiling. He turned back to Kevin. "This just might be my lucky day. I was here with some friends and they had to unexpectedly leave. Could you give me a ride home?"

Kevin glanced at Amy and she nodded. "Amy's driving, but sure. We were just getting ready to leave."

"Thank you," Jake said, seeming very grateful. Amy and Kevin got up from the table and they all headed out of the restaurant.

+++

Tara was torn. She didn't know if she could go out on their movie night and act like everything was normal. What bothered her even more was she really was jealous of Kevin and Amy going on a date, and she had no reason to feel that way. She finally picked up her cell phone and typed in a text message to Kevin.

Tara: Hey Kev, not feeling well. Just gonna stay home. Maybe next month.

She put her cell phone down and stared at it, as if waiting for it to miraculously chime that he had left a reply. After several minutes of sitting there and seeing no response, she turned on the television and unmuted it, then laid back and sprawled out on the couch. She was wearing her lounge pants and a tank top, already dressed for bed. The time alone was good, although she was not looking forward to hearing about his date. She flipped through channels, until she came across a station that said Breaking News. She turned it up, stopping on the channel.

"Another grizzly murder has taken place today. We are reporting live on the corner of Broderick and Schaeffer Street, where the body of 23 year old Derek Jeffries was discovered in the woods two hours ago. He was reported missing forty-eight hours earlier. There are no suspects, as of yet. However, the police has asked the public to come forward if they witnessed anything that night. One eye witness has reported that she saw a man with a red hoodie and the trim of a blue baseball cap coming out of the woods, just an hour before the body was discovered. The witness was not able to recall any other information about the identity of the possible suspect. Reporting live, this is Parker Jacobs."

Tara turned the television off. She couldn't believe that another murder had been committed so soon. Their small town had rarely experienced any violent crimes in the 22 years she had grown up there. In fact, she couldn't recall a time that there was ever a killing. She heard the doorbell and got up to answer it. When she opened up the door, Kevin stood gawking at her.

He looked her up and down. "It doesn't appear you are ready to go to the movies."

"Didn't you get the message? I'm not going. I sent you a text," she replied, moving away from the door.

He stepped into the house. "I got your message, but I didn't think you were being serious. I know how much you want to go to this movie. It's a romantic comedy...isn't it?"

She heaved a sigh, "Yes, but..."

"You have no reason not to go." Again he looked her up and down, "Other than the fact you are dressed for bed, but you can fix that quickly. Come on, I want to take you."

She groaned, frustrated. "Whatever," she said. "Give me ten minutes." She hurried up the stairs and into her bedroom. She looked in her closet and finally settled on a simple University of Alaska t-shirt and a pair of jean shorts. She brushed her hair quickly, and headed back downstairs.

"So how was your date yesterday?" She asked with some sarcasm.

He laughed, turning to her before opening the front door. "Tell me the truth. That really bothered you, didn't it?" She was thrown by his question and searched for an answer.

She rolled her eyes, "It didn't bother me. I just..." she paused, knowing that she wasn't telling him the truth. "Maybe it bothered me a little bit," she hesitated, "but, just a little bit."

He laughed, "I'll take that." He waited on the porch for her to lock up, and put his arm over her shoulders as they headed to his car. "Let's just put it this way. After yesterday, I am sure that Amy knows where we stand." He opened the door for her and she met his eyes.

"Is that so?" she asked, smiling.

"It's possible that I might have mentioned your name a couple of times during the conversation."

"A couple?"

"Five...six times max, but that's all."

She snickered, getting into the car. She felt relieved, but all the more curious to hear how it went.

+++

Sitting in the theatre next to her, Kevin found it difficult to ignore his feelings for Tara. He regretted not telling her how he felt. It probably wasn't a good idea to go to a romantic comedy movie with her. As the actor and actress were making out on the big screen, he pictured them as the two in the starring roles. He glanced at her out of the corner of his eye and he could see that she was probably uncomfortable as well.

At one point, he even swore she groaned next to him. It caused him to perk up and he was becoming more aware of his erection pressing against his zipper. He shifted his body in his chair, but nothing seemed to help. He reached his hand into the popcorn container, trying to take his mind off of it. Yet, the only thing that happened was his hand grazed across hers. He froze for a moment and then allowed his fingers to slowly stroking hers. He was longing to touch her and he hoped that he was reading her signs correctly.

His fingers traced hers up and down and their eyes met. The moment their eyes connected, she was torn from the trance. She pulled her hand out of the bucket and turned back to the movie screen. The moment was lost.

He tried to turn back to the screen and watch what was going on, but the couple on the screen was now doing more than kissing. He moaned as he saw their foreplay, knowing a sex scene was imminent. This was going to be too much to take. He just knew it. He shifted again in his seat, accidentally brushing her leg. His hand trailed down her bare leg and instead of quickly pulling away, he allowed it to linger. What was even more of a shocker was that she didn't try to move away.

As his hand slid back up her leg, he let his fingers slip past the seam of her shorts, gently grazing her thigh. Their eyes met and she made no attempt to stop him. He drifted up a tad more, feeling the silk of her panties and then falling back. His hand pulled out from under her shorts and he felt himself getting sweaty. They never looked away from each other. He watched her intently, as she moved her hand toward him and then rubbed over his throbbing cock. He moaned, closing his eyes and taking a deep breath. He opened his eyes to find her staring at him. She appeared lost in the moment, as was he.

Her eyes widened, as she gently ran her hand against him. He took a chance, moving closer to her. They were only inches from kissing, but he wasn't sure how she would react. She turned and leaned closer to him, welcoming him in. He still hesitated, because there was so much uncertainty. He didn't want to hurt their friendship. Her hand had released from his manhood, but he still had the memory of her hand stroking him through his jeans.

Her breathing was heavy, and suddenly, nothing seemed to matter more than connecting his lips to hers. His right arm wrapped around her, pulling her to him, while his left hand went down and lifted the cup holder that was between them. She shifted her body, moving closer to him as he ran his hands down her back. His tongue dove into her mouth, grazing over hers. His heart was beating so loudly, as he had held off on showing her how he felt for so long. He pulled away slightly, but continued to gently nibble at her lower lip. He didn't want the moment to end and he had no intention of parting from their embrace.

Tara was nervous, but relieved Kevin had finally made the first move. His touch along her leg had sent a wave of pent up desire through her body, and his kiss took her breath away. As he pulled from the kiss to nibble on her lip, she still wanted more. She let her tongue trail over his lips and then slipped back inside.

A gentle moan escaped her, causing him to intensify the kiss. Her arms wrapped around his waist she slipped her hands up under his t-shirt. She dug her nails into his back, causing him to wince with pleasure and desire.

Kevin felt Tara's nails dig into his back and it drove him wild. He slid his tongue in and out of her mouth, claiming her in the dark theatre. He could hear the sound of the actors making love on the movie screen was heard, but he couldn't tear himself away from her. This embrace was everything that he had been waiting for.

+++

Hidden in the last row of the movie theatre, a pair of eyes were watching them. He couldn't believe that they were making out like this, where everyone could see them. He was disgusted by their blatant disregard for his feelings. He groaned, agitated that they could betray him like this.

Anger darkened his eyes. He was the guy for Tara and the sooner she figured that out, the better off everyone would be. He stood up, unable to watch any more of their charade. It was a spectacle that he wanted nothing to do with. Tara was his, and he swore he would make them both pay.

END OF SAMPLE

The Wild Flames Series is coming soon. Be sure to sign up for my exclusive reader list at www.bellalovewins.com to be advised of its release.

27503622R00094

Made in the USA
San Bernardino, CA
13 December 2015